Christmas Bells

by

Linda Joyce

Christmas Bells

Contact Information: info@wordworkspress.com

Cover Art by EJR Digital Art

Published by:
Word Works Press, LLC
P.O. Box 625
Acworth, GA 30101
Visit Word Works Press at
http://www.wordworkspress.com

Publishing History
Print Book ISBN-13:978-0-9965811-6-5
Digital ISBN-13:978-0-9965811-5-8

Awards

Bayou Born – 2014 RONE Award Finalist
1st Honorable Mention—Contemporary Romance
Novel from Oklahoma Writers' Federation Inc.

Bayou Bound – 2015 RONE Award Finalist
& 1st Place in Romance from
Southeastern Writers Association

Bayou Beckons – 2016 RONE Award Finalist
Best of 2015 Contemporary Women's Fiction from
Authors on the Air Book Reviewers

Her Heart's Desire – 2016 RONE Award Finalist
1st Place in Romance from
Southeastern Writers Association

Other Books by Linda Joyce

Fleur de Lis Series:
Bayou Born

Bayou Bound

Bayou Beckons

Coming soon: Bayou Brides

Sunflower Series
Her Heart's Desire

Novella
Behind The Mask

Coming Soon!
Fleur de Lis Brides series
BRANNA December 7, 2016
BILOXI January 11, 2017
CAMILLA February 15, 2017

Dedication

Christmas Bells is dedicated to Avery R.

I met Avery at physical therapy. She inspired me with her intelligence, charm, and perseverance. She epitomizes my husband's words:
"Challenges are blessings in disguise."

A few words
from Linda…

Thank you for selecting *Christmas Bells* as one of your reads. I enjoy connecting with booklovers. Please let me hear from you about how you enjoy this story. I invite you to leave a review at a book retail website if you love *Christmas Bells*.

A few years back, I severely sprained my ankle, which left me hopping around with crutches for three months. Afterward, I entered physical therapy to regain the strength and muscle I'd lost. While there, I met a girl about eight years old. She inspired me to write *Cupid's Arrow*, a short story published in a now-defunct magazine.

At the beginning of 2016, USA Today and Amazon Bestselling author, Ciara Knight, invited to me participate in an anthology. Twelve authors… twelve stories… connected in some way to dyslexia. The anthology was a fundraiser for Gracepoint School, a school for dyslexic learners which gives students the tools to transition to the public school system. Inspired by Ms. Knight, an award-winning author with dyslexia, I wanted to be a part of the project. This is when I merged the short story about Avery and the fundraiser together. Though *Christmas Bells* is definitely a different story, Avery—the glue in the story—is still the same. She does not have dyslexia; however, she still continues to persevere through her own situation.

Thank you, Avery, for continuing to inspire me. I know you inspire others, too.

I am humbled and grateful to be a part of the *Love & Grace* anthology, and I extend my thanks to Ciara Knight. It's been a wonderful team experience.

I don't take anything in my writing world for granted. I appreciate the support of my editor, Cheryl Walz. She lives in Chicago, but her roots are in Georgia, and she gets my southern quirks.

Due to last minute changes, I am very grateful for Elle at EJR Digital Art. She stepped in to help me out by creating this beautiful cover. I love her designs.

Brenda White at *Formatting Done Wright* has lifted a burden from my shoulders. You have my gratitude. Thank you!

To Poised Pen Productions for all the support—ALL the support. Teresa Russ, I am very blessed that you are my friend.

To Linda's Lovelies, I am forever grateful for your friendship and continued support. I appreciate that you're willing to share this journey with me, cheering me on along the way, especially given all that's happened this with my family.

2016 has been a very difficult year. My mother became very sick in January, and then she passed away in May. Following her, Renoir and Gentleman Jack, two of my fur-baby boys, crossed the Rainbow Bridge in June. Through the loving support of friends, I have managed to move forward. I can't express the depth of my gratitude for the support. Thank you.

Last, but never least, I thank my husband, Don, for his support. My ability to write and grow as an author would not be possible without your constant encouragement. We are two hearts that beat as one.

Please consider supporting Gracepoint by purchasing a copy of *Love & Grace*. 100% of all sales go to the school.

Christmas Bells

Chapter One

Tapping two fingers to her bottom lip, Morgan scanned the studio kitchen at the television station. Bright spotlights brought every item on the cooking island into sharp focus. Her set needed a few personal touches before today's shoot of *Cooking with Kids*. Had she healed enough to bring that sentimental item out of storage? Maybe.

Her crew had decorated the set professionally with a winter theme, but it still needed something special. A feature item. The perfect statement piece, handmade locally, waited tucked in the back of the prop room. The kids on her show would love it, not to mention it would be new to many of her viewers, since the last time it graced a set was three years ago.

Bryce had presented it to her when he crashed the taping of the holiday show dressed in a Santa suit complete with bulky belly padding. She wanted to be mad at him for ruining her timing on the show, but his infectious "Ho! Ho! Ho!" put

1

everyone in stitches. She'd married a crazy man, the perfect complement to her all-too-serious nature. That memory about him was now one of her favorites.

She remembered the day as though it happened only a week ago…and she wished she hadn't wasted even a single minute being irritated with him. Regret, she'd learned the hard way, was like an anchor weighing her down. After years of grieving and finally moving out of depression, she promised herself she would truly embrace living. So it was now or never. At least for the holiday decoration tucked out of sight.

"I'll be back in a second, Corinna," she told her younger assistant. Her heels clicked on the polished concrete floor. The *tap-tap* sounded confident and upbeat to her ears, more evidence of her returning happiness. She made her way to the closet beyond the brightness of the set in search of the conical-shaped tree made from oyster shells. It would add the perfect southern touch to the table and bring in a visual element of height. Mentioning the Savannah artist who created the piece on her show would hopefully be a boon for his holiday sales.

She slid a box across the floor to keep the door ajar. Confined spaces still made her a bit anxious, something that began three years ago. Everything changed her back then in a single day. Now, trying to shake off panicky sensations of walls closing in, she shook out her hands and reminded herself, "Breathe."

Calmness settled over her nerves a few breaths later and allowed her to continue the hunt.

Ambient light from the set lit the long narrow room. She spotted the item she sought covered in plastic. It was perched high on a shelf and would require a ladder and some assistance to get it down.

2

As she was about to call out for her assistant, she heard a voice from within the studio say, "Hey, Corinna."

Morgan waited for the newcomer to finish her business.

"Tina, I'm working." Corinna sounded annoyed.

Morgan didn't recognize the woman's voice, but Corinna had proven herself capable over the last year and could handle anything, so Morgan redirected her attention to various items in storage. A six-foot wooden heart she'd used at Valentine's Day leaned against the back wall. With a bit of work, lights could be added to give it a refreshed look. Red, white, and blue banners for the 4th of July needed replacing. A beach-ball-sized pumpkin for Halloween was a new acquisition a couple of months back. Stroking the orange velvety surface, she stopped when she heard the tinkling of a little boy's laughter. She glanced from side to side and waited, but the sound didn't return. It came from nowhere and seemed to evaporate in the air. Lasted long enough to capture her attention, but never lasting as long as she wanted to hear it. While the sound used to make her sad, now it wrapped her in a deep feeling of motherly love.

"I just wanted to tell you. I have a *date*." The woman made it sound as though a date was on par with hitting the lottery.

"Date?"

"Alexander Blake. Score the big time for me."

Hearing Alex's name, Morgan moved closer to the open door and eavesdropped on the conversation.

"Tina," Corinna snapped. "This is a place of business, not a dating service. I got you the job as an intern to help you out. *Do not* embarrass me. Besides, he's too old for you."

Corinna's harsh admonishment was surprising.

3

"It's business." Tina's words dripped sweetly. "His company does the station's advertising, and I just happen to work in the marketing department. It's a perfect fit. We're going to discuss a new campaign for next year. Over lunch."

"That's not a date. I'll tell you now. He's not interested in you."

Satisfied that Corinna had the conversation well in hand, Morgan reached for a green felt-covered box. She hadn't looked inside it for three years. Maybe this year the pain had finally lessened enough for her to find joy in opening the box again. She'd brought it to work to hide it. The pain of storing it at home was just too much.

"How can you be so sure?" Tina's voice took on an accusatory tone.

"Because the only time his eyes light up, since his wife died, is when Morgan walks into the room."

Morgan's heart quickened.

What had Corinna just said?

No. She and Alex were friends. He was Avery's father. No, Corinna couldn't be right about him.

"But she's *old*," Tina whined. "She's like thirty-two or something."

That's old?

"Ms. Marshall isn't old. And Mr. Blake is thirty-five," Corinna shot back.

"So what's a dozen years between soul mates?"

Corinna snorted. "Soul mates? No, darlin', you're mistaken. We both know you're looking for a sugar daddy. Besides, the man has a daughter he adores, and *you* are not stepmother material. Not in this lifetime, anyway."

Morgan straightened and pushed her dark brown hair

4

behind her ears. Clearly, Corinna paid attention to those around her if she noticed all the things she told the other woman.

"Want to bet how long it takes *me* to get him into bed?"

Alarms clanged in Morgan's head. Her heart fluttered like the wings of a panicky bird. She'd heard enough. "Corinna? Would you mind helping me in here?"

Surprised at her reaction to the dialogue taking place out of sight, Morgan pursed her lips. It was none of her business what this Tina person did or with whom. Nor was Alex's private life any of her concern... Except she liked him as a friend. Admired him as a gentleman. After all, he had been devoted to his wife who passed more than a year ago, and his daughter Avery held a special place in her heart.

The sweet girl was a regular on her show and came to her house weekly for cooking lessons as part of an afterschool group. The eight-year-old girl with the dimples, smiling brown eyes, and fawn-colored hair captured her heart the first time they'd met. She was the same age as her son…or the age her son would've been if he had survived.

Chapter Two

Alex stood at the window of his fourth-floor office, phone to his ear, listening to his mother's voice message. He gazed at the people enjoying the mild winter weather in Johnson Square, one of the twenty-two historic squares in Savannah, Georgia, the city of his family for generations. Except that, at that moment, his parents weren't in residence, in fact, not even stateside. It was his own fault they were vacationing in Europe for three weeks in December. Waiting for them to return was like waiting to spot Rudolph and his fellow reindeer in the sky on Christmas Eve.

"Alexander, honey, we're going to Austria today." His mother's voice sounded breathlessly excited. "We're having such a good time. Although, this time zone difference has turned me around like revolving door. Hope I didn't wake you."

He saved the message before ending the call as a reminder

he'd made the right decision to give them their Christmas present early despite his wish for their return. Seeing Europe lit up for Christmas was the top of their bucket list. They needed to enjoy it while they could. No one knew what tomorrow would hold... The adage of not putting off important things hit home when his wife died suddenly from pneumonia eighteen months ago, a complication from her treatment for cancer.

This year, for the first time in his life, he would undertake December traditions without his mom or his wife overseeing everything. He was a topnotch elf, and would do as instructed, but he didn't have the eye for all the extra details. Like coming up with an original theme for decorating the Christmas tree. White lights only, twinkle on a timer, or blinking? What about a mixture of red, green, and white lights? Then there was the selecting and buying of different wrapping paper for each person in the family—his mother insisted on it each year for as long as he could remember, and his wife had considered it a brilliant idea.

The holiday to-do list was daunting enough, but managing life *and* the holidays...insane. He couldn't wait for his parents' plane to taxi to the gate at the Jacksonville airport. After the last five days of juggling his schedule, plus melding his daughter's school and social calendar, he wondered how his mother managed it—more importantly, would *he* survive fatherhood?

Never before had a Friday held as much appeal as it did today. He couldn't wait for the day to be over. A pizza and a cold beer tonight would remind him of his less complicated years.

"Knock, knock." Emma, his secretary, entered his office. "Boss, you need to leave for that lunch meeting with the TV station staff. As in, leave now. Also, don't forget Avery's choir program tonight. Do you need me to have a car pick her up from school today? You wanted me to remind you to buy a Christmas tree tomorrow."

"You still think I need a fresh tree this year? It's not like my mother can object. It will be a done deal by the time she gets back on the 23rd." Alex sighed. Emma proved to be efficient and helpful over the five years since he hired her, taking a chance on her drive though she had no real experience. She and her husband had provided a great deal of support since his wife, Casey, had died, making last Christmas a somber affair. This year, he wanted to restore joy to the holiday, most importantly for Avery's sake, and Emma helped him stay on track.

"Don't even go there again. A fake tree? No." She handed him a slip of paper with an address. "That's the place to get the tree. Your mother will kill me if she finds an artificial tree in her house."

"We're decorating my house this year, not hers. She agreed."

Emma grabbed his suit coat from the hook behind the door and motioned him out of his office. "Go. Now. To make life easier, I'll have Avery delivered here when school gets out. Then you can have a nice father-daughter dinner before her program tonight. We'll see you there."

How had he ended up with so many bossy women in his life? At least, Casey, crafty woman that she'd been, had a way of finessing him to do things. Emma just ordered him around. His mother used her southern charm, a smile, a lilting laugh, and her deadly raised eyebrow to keep him in line. All of them had his best interest at heart, thankfully.

"I'm going." His grouse sounded harsher than he intended. He snatched his coat and scooped up the folder on his desk. As he crossed the threshold, he turned back to Emma who was straightening up his desk. "I do appreciate you, just in case you were wondering." He smiled at her.

"I know you do. When I think you don't, I remind you what a fabulous secretary you have." Her impish grin let him know he was back in her good graces.

Driving to Harbor Grill for lunch, he wondered how Peter, the head of the public relations department, liked the new campaign his firm proposed. It was more contemporary than in the past. Over the last five years, he and Peter had been on the same page. They both wanted tasteful quality advertising when presenting the station to the public. However, this time, the commercials projected a hip and edgier vibe to capture a younger audience. Did Peter like the latest ideas, or was the reason for lunch away from the office a pretext for delivering bad news in private?

He arrived at the restaurant exactly on time. The hostess led him to a table covered with a crisp white linen tablecloth.

"Hello, Mr. Blake." Ms. Ward, the intern from the marketing department, waited alone at a table set for two by the window.

"Hello." He glanced at the table and then back at her.

"Hey there." She tilted her head slightly to one side and smiled, holding out her hand, wrist bent and palm down. He wondered if she expected him to kiss it rather than shake it. After setting a folder on the table, he reached for her hand, clasped it in both of his, and then gave it a couple of pumps before releasing it.

"It's nice to see you again, Ms. Ward."

Where the heck was Peter?

"Why, Alex, I thought we'd moved past formalities. Call me Tina, please." She raked her fingers through her hair and shook her head slightly, flipping her hair over her shoulders.

He was pretty rusty, but if he didn't know better, he'd think Ms. Tina Ward was flirting with him. She was certainly attractive, the kind of woman who stood out in a crowd, and everything about her said expensive and demanding from the highlights in her hair to the manicured nails and diamond bracelet. He appreciated her appeal the way he appreciated a fine piece of art—nice to look at, but he couldn't afford it, and even if he could, he wouldn't want it hanging in his home.

When she dipped her chin and looked up at him, his discernment went on high alert. If he wasn't careful, things might take a wrong turn. He remembered Morse Code from his Boy Scout days, but female code…not his forte. "Are we waiting for Peter?"

She shook her head. "No, today it's just me."

Taking a seat across the table from her, he motioned the waiter over.

"What would you like to drink?" Alex asked her as the waiter stood slightly bent, eager to grant her any request. He wanted the young man to put his eyes back in his head.

"I'll have sparkling water with a twist of lime." She reached across the table and placed her hand on his side of the table. "But once I get your new advertising plan approved, I'll let you buy me champagne."

"I'll have a glass of water and a cup of decaf with my lunch," he told the waiter as her words registered in his mind. "When the plan is approved, I'll throw a party for the department at the station. Cater the food. Do they allow alcohol

10

at the station now?"

"Well…" She batted her lashes and smiled coyly. "I had a more intimate affair in mind." She stroked her fingers on the tablecloth as though giving him a preview of her invitation.

"Ah…that would…be…interesting. Would you excuse me, please?" He sounded like an awkward college boy. It hadn't been since those days that a woman had flirted so outrageously with him. Heading for the men's room, he pulled out his phone and voice-texted Emma.

Call Peter. Tactfully ask about changes in his department's procedures. As in—is there anything new I need to know before pitching our newest campaign to him? Check my schedule. Invite him for drinks at the marina where he docks his boat. Then call me in ten minutes with an emergency. I've got to get out of here.

"Shall we order?" he asked Tina when he returned to the table. A second later, the waiter appeared with their beverages and rattled off the lunch specials. She ordered crab salad. He ordered a sandwich with fries he had no intention of eating.

"I'm a little surprised," she said.

He raised an eyebrow and waited for her to explain.

"You're clearly someone who works out regularly. And you eat French fries. I like a man who knows what he wants and goes for it."

He forced a smile. She was being about as subtle as sunshine on a sunny day. But he didn't want to insult her or embarrass her in any way.

Ring. Ring.

He pulled his phone from his jacket pocket. "I'm sorry," he told her. "I have to take this."

She nodded in understanding.

11

"Hello, Emma."

"Avery called. She doesn't feel well. I spoke to the school nurse, and she wants to send Avery home."

"Yes, I understand. I'll leave here immediately."

"Alex, this is not the emergency you asked me for. This is the *real* thing."

"Okay," he said slowly, his mind latching on to the news with alarm. His pulse raced. Avery hadn't been sick a day since her mother had passed away. "I'll leave now." Looking across the table at Tina, he patted her hand. "I'm very sorry to do this, but I have to cut our lunch short. My daughter is sick at school—"

"I would love to meet Avery. Shall I come with you?"

She knows my daughter's name? He paused. Tina's persistence was more than a little bold. "I think it would better for you to meet her another time." He turned to get the waiter's attention.

"I love children," Tina gushed.

"Sir, how may I help you?" the waiter asked.

"I need to pay the check. I have an emergency and must leave."

"Right away, sir."

Alex stood. "I'll have my secretary contact you to set up another time for a meeting. My firm is ready to *wow* the station. Please give Peter my best regards."

"Of course," she said brightly. "I hope we can wrap up this deal before the end of the year. What better way to ring in the New Year than with a new campaign in place?"

Alex nodded and smiled. How could he respond to the question when he wasn't quite sure what kind of deal she had in mind?

As he stepped from the restaurant to the sidewalk, he called the school nurse, who surely would call an ambulance if Avery was in any serious distress. After answering his call, the woman gave him vague answers, and then he asked to speak to his daughter.

"Daddy, you're coming to get me now, right?" Avery wailed.

The pained whine in her voice caused his pulse to skyrocket. "Yes, Sugar. I'll be there in a few minutes. What's wrong?"

"Stomachache. Bad. I want to go home. Please hurry, Daddy."

"Hold tight. Daddy's coming." God help him if she was sick because of the breakfast he'd made for her. A bacon and peanut butter sandwich. She'd insisted, and he complied. He wanted to prevent any morning drama that might carry over and hinder her evening performance. He'd even let her walk halfway to school when she insisted rather than dropping her at the front as he or his mother did most mornings. He'd trailed behind to make sure she made it to school unharmed.

Stalking toward the parking garage, he couldn't remember any illnesses Avery had suffered. No chicken pox or measles. No mumps or even whooping cough. The worst affliction she'd suffered beside a cold was the stomach flu—one time. Being sick was when she needed a mother…and when he wished for a caring woman in their lives to help guide him. His mother doted on Avery, nearly to the point of smothering. But she didn't like craft projects—she hated to mess up her nails—nor did she know about contemporary music or kayaking, two of Avery's favorite things.

Ring. Ring.

"Yes, Emma." Alex started his car. "I'm headed to pick up Avery."

"I think it's a case of the nerves," his secretary said. "I think Avery is scared to sing her solo tonight."

"What? I don't understand. She's been singing on stages since she was four. She didn't mention that. She said her stomach hurt."

"Talk to her calmly. You'll figure it out. Just don't go rushing over there, blowing stoplights, and causing any accidents. I think she'll be fine."

He sighed. "Her voice sounded scared. It shook me. Thanks for letting me know. Now my heart won't pump out of my chest."

After making it safely through several intersections on green lights, he caught a red one a block from the school. Waiting for the light to change, he drummed his fingers on the steering wheel.

He wanted his daughter to grow up with a mother, but life took an unexpected turn and robbed them of the anchor in their life. But he also wanted a wife. A woman who would bring love and laughter to him *and* Avery. His mother had been encouraging him to consider dating. Even raised that eyebrow at him the last time he scoffed at her suggestion. She'd be shocked to learn he had given the idea some thought lately. But when he attempted to make a list of women he would consider, only one name had come to mind. She had beauty and brains. Beauty in that wholesome woman-next-door kind of way, not the drenched-in-makeup-and-jewelry kind of woman several of his friends had married. High maintenance wasn't his thing. Her inward beauty shone, too. It was revealed in her kindness and patience with kids. Her laughter was lilting and captivating. Her smile heartwarming. Her conversation was informed and stimulating. She could tell a good story.

He'd met Morgan Marshall during a fundraising event for the television station about three years ago. Unlike most other TV personalities he'd met, she drew people in, more interested in finding out about others than boasting about herself. She exuded a quiet grace and radiated an inner strength. He'd offered his condolences back when he heard about her tragedy. She politely thanked him, and they'd never spoken of it again.

Yet, she always talked eagerly about Avery with him, ever since his daughter started taking her afternoon cooking class. Most recently, her eyes danced with delight when she told him about his daughter's accomplishments with food.

Yeah, he'd made a list of women he was interested in. A waste of paper. A list of one. And then he had completely dismissed it.

When the light finally changed, Alex spotted a red SUV. He waved. Morgan waved back. Would she be surprised to learn he had just been thinking of her? Her friendship was important, not only to him, but Avery, too. Morgan had shown his daughter great compassion since Casey died. She even helped Avery with her schoolwork whenever he arrived late to collect his child from the cooking class. She inspired his little girl to keep trying. He couldn't think of a better woman to be part of Avery's life.

"Dyslexia isn't a prison sentence," she'd told Avery, "but a challenge to overcome for the world to see how special you are. Whatever else may happen, you can never give up."

After that, Avery sang Morgan's praises every week after cooking class. Not only was his child gaining an understanding about cooking, but also about where food came from and how to tackle recipes.

He wanted to know Morgan better. Her energy sparkled and a magnetism drew him to her, but he feared the problems a date would create if she didn't like him well enough after the first one to join him on a second one. Her relationship with his daughter ranked higher than his needs. Avery had to come first.

But a daydream about Morgan now and then couldn't hurt anything, he hoped.

Chapter Three

Morgan arrived home. Excitement tingled through her body. Her heart beat with fluttering lightness, a new experience since Bryce and Justin had died. With a gentle grip, she carried a brand new box with a treasure into the kitchen. This year, she looked forward to actually finishing her holiday decorating, unlike the past two years. Memories lifted her up with joy like a bright star shining in a clear night sky, rather than plummeting her into dark sadness.

Gingerly taking a crystal bell from a red velvet-lined box, her newest addition to the collection, she placed it on the top shelf of the treasured wooden stand Bryce had purchased the first year they were married. Round ball feet supported a wide circular base with three shelves. From the base upward, each shelf grew smaller. The top one could hold a single bell. The entire stand resembled the shape of a Christmas tree, and it greeted everyone who entered her front door from its perch on the mahogany antique table in the foyer.

Gazing at the bell, she walked around the display to observe it from different angles. This new bell was different from all the others. Larger, with a faceted crystal clapper. Hundreds of sparkling tiny crystals covered the upper portion of the bell. It was a special edition by a famous crystal company. She'd spied it in the window of a jewelry store after lunching with one of her cousins. Somehow, it triggered her desire to decorate again, and she had to have it. Her cousin had staunchly reminded her that decorations were just things. Developing an attachment to them or assigning them any emotional value was just not appropriate.

But she couldn't help it. The bell whispered to her. It was beautifully made, ornate, and unique. Her hands went to her chest as she stared, breathing in joy and serenity, emotions she had worried would be lost to her forever.

"I hope you love it as much as I do," she whispered. "It's in honor of you."

The tinkling laughter of a boy floated for a brief moment in the room. Morgan smiled, comforted by the sound. "Thank you."

Walking to the living room to turn on Christmas music, she noticed the flashing light on her home phone. Only work and her cooking students called that number. Everyone else used her cell phone. Urgency pushing her, Morgan reached for the phone, punched in the code, and waited for a message.

"Miss Morgan, this is Avery Blake. Could I talk to you? Please call me back." That was twenty minutes ago. A long time to an eight-year-old. The plea in the girl's whispered message alarmed her.

Hitting redial, she called the Blake home.

"Hello?"

"This is Morgan Marshall. May I speak with Avery, please?"

"Oh, thank God," Alex said. "I don't know what to do. Avery's crying. My mother usually handles her tears, but she's away on a trip in Europe. Besides, my daughter says she only wants to talk to you. That you'll understand."

"Is she sick? Running a fever? Did something happen?"

"Honestly, her vital signs are normal. But the tears...You have to help me."

Alex's anxiety surprised her. He always projected a calm and relaxed demeanor. "Could I speak with her?"

"Avery, Sugar, Daddy has Miss Morgan on the phone."

A heart-wrenching sob came through the phone's speaker, followed by wailing, "Daddy, I...*hiccup*...want to *see* her."

"If you can't come here," Alex said in a rush, "then I'll bring her to you. *Anything* to calm my child. Her tears make my heart hurt. Her sobs are stabbing me like swords. She's been this way since I picked her up from school."

"I'll be over as fast as it takes for me to drive there." Morgan grabbed her purse. "Tell Avery I'm on my way."

"Thank you." Never before had she heard a man sound so relieved.

Morgan drove five blocks to the Blake residence, worry pushing her along. She hadn't met Avery until after five-year-old Justin died. Soon after, she discovered that she and the girl shared something significant. While she couldn't protect Avery from the pitfalls of her condition, she could help her cope with the misunderstanding arising from the ignorance of others.

Gripping the steering, Morgan squeezed the wheel tighter and focused on the road. Treelined streets. Manicured landscapes. The angle of the afternoon sun cast long shadows. The neighborhood changed as she traveled the short distance between her house and Avery's. Single-story cottages dotted her neighborhood, but the style of the houses changed the closer she got to the Blake home. They lived in a large, brick two-story colonial. Pulling sharply onto the driveway, she parked.

Alex opened the door before she pressed the doorbell. "Up there. Door on the right." He pointed.

She shoved her purse at him when a sob tore through the silence of the house. As she bounded up the wooden stairs, her steps were muffled by a wool runner.

"Avery, I'm here." Morgan thrust open the door. A girl's room covered in pink. On the floor, her back to her bed, knees and head bent, hands covering her head, the girl's body shook as she cried harder.

Rushing to her side, Morgan sank down beside Avery, pulling her over on her side, resting Avery's head in her lap. "Oh, Avery." She whispered her name over and over as she stroked her hair. "Tell me what's wrong."

Avery sniffed and fought to catch her breath. "She— she—she said, I was…stupid."

Morgan's heart seized. "Who said that?" She had been on the receiving end of that kind of bullying when she was a kid. "You and I know that's not true." Children with dyslexia were often singled out and cruelly labeled.

"But—but—I have to *work* so hard…to—to learn new words…when I read."

"That makes you brave and smart. You're strong. You don't give up," Morgan whispered. "Who said this about you?"

"Penelope Hiller."

Morgan was well acquainted with the Hiller family. The girl's mother, a socialite with more money than all the Christmas lights in Savannah, bragged on her daughter, but rarely spent time with her. Nannies and drivers cared for the girl. Penelope's father ran a shipping company. He also ran around, not so discreetly, on his wife. He'd even tried to seduce Morgan after her husband died. The scumbag. Sadly, Penelope paid the price for neglect from her parents.

"That little miss is not an expert on anything. You're special. She's jealous because you have a solo tonight, and she doesn't."

"But," Avery wailed, sitting up to face her. "She said I sing like a bellowing cow."

Morgan laughed. "Oh baby, I doubt Penelope's ever even heard a bellowing cow. You're a sweet, angelic soprano. A bellow is a deep masculine sound. They're nothing alike. She's just trying to throw you off your game. Ignore her."

Avery sniffed and raised her eyebrows as though she wanted to believe, but couldn't quite get there.

"Trust me on this." Morgan began planning the conversation she would have with Mrs. Hiller, one the socialite wasn't likely to forget. How would Mrs. Hiller feel if her darling Penelope never got another slot on the *Cooking with Kids* show?

Avery held on to her. Her sniffles lessened. Patiently, Morgan waited for the girl to sort out her feelings.

When Alex appeared in the doorway, Morgan shooed him away with a flick of her hand. She continued to stroke Avery's hair. "How about a cup of warm tea? Do you want something to eat before your performance?"

"Not now."

Avery's breathing soon returned to normal. She looked up. "I think Daddy wants to go out to eat. Mimi isn't here to cook, and Daddy isn't so hot in the kitchen."

Sitting up, Avery faced Morgan and cocked her head. "Hey, I'm pretty funny. It's hot in the kitchen when Daddy's trying to cook. He's good at burning things."

Morgan rose and stretched out her arm to Avery. "How about you show your daddy some of your cooking skills? Let him know he's getting something with the hard-earned money he's paying me to teach you every week. I'll be your sous chef. Let's go raid the fridge."

The smile spreading across Avery's sweet face was worth more to her than all the diamonds Mrs. Hiller owned. Morgan pulled the girl tightly into a big hug. If she had a daughter, she'd want her to be just as sweet, kind, and smart as Avery.

Holding hands, they descended the stairs. Alex rose from the bottom step and looked up at them. The furrow of his brow disappeared as he leaned against the newel post. "Ladies, may I take you to dinner?"

"No, Daddy. I'm going to cook for you."

Alex's gaze connected with Morgan's. His warm brown eyes twinkled. A little flutter started deep in her chest. As the fluttering increased, she glanced away.

"What doesn't kill you makes you stronger." She smiled at him instead of telling him to trust Avery.

When the girl reached the bottom of the stairs, she ran for the kitchen. "Come watch me, Daddy."

Morgan started to follow, but stopped when Alex touched her arm. "You're sure about this." He tilted his head toward the kitchen. Uncertainty filled his eyes.

"Oh ye of little faith," Morgan admonished teasingly.

22

"Your daughter can cook a four-star meal. Just you wait and see."

"Well, Miss Morgan, if my child gives me food poisoning, I'm going to hold you responsible. I'll insist you nurse me back to health." He winked and then bowed, waving his hand in a flourish, suggesting he would follow her lead to the kitchen.

Morgan took a step, stopped, and glanced over her shoulder. Alex was grinning wider than she'd ever seen. The slightly crinkled, starched white shirt with the cuffs rolled up, top button undone, tucked into charcoal gray slacks made his chest appear broader, his waist slimmer, and his smile brighter. She had never noticed the strength in the squareness of his jaw or the thickness of his lashes. A tingle shivered along her spine. Was the man flirting with her?

"Tell me what you need me to do," Alex said once they were all in the kitchen.

"Set the table, of course," Avery piped up. "You do what I normally do, and I'll do what Miss Morgan does—cook."

Morgan put together a bowl of salad from the items Avery pulled from the refrigerator—cucumber, apple slices, and dried cranberries. She helped slice sweet potatoes into chips for baking after they were peeled. Without a word of instruction, she kept an eye on Avery as the girl melted butter to sauté shrimp. Avery's mother had a dream kitchen. Everything exactly in a perfect place, but sadly, the room would fit better in a showroom than in a house. She'd heard that Casey rarely cooked. Why would someone want a dream kitchen and then not use it? She spied a binder at the end of the counter with take-out menus that had seen more use than the kitchen.

When they sat down to eat, Avery asked, "For dessert,

how about ice cream with sprinkles?"

"You're going to make ice cream, too?" Alex asked. "Wow. I'm feeling extra pampered tonight. Two beautiful ladies *and* ice cream after dinner. But first, we say grace."

"No, Daddy." Avery laughed. "You're going to buy us ice cream on our way to my recital."

"I see. Then I have even more to be thankful for." Alex bowed his head. Avery and Morgan followed. He offered thanks for the meal and threw in a word of gratitude for friends willing to help at the drop of a hat. Morgan smiled at his not-so-subtle hint.

After the last "Amen," Morgan said, "We could wait and have hot chocolate and a brownie at my house after your performance. The kind with cream cheese and the fudge frosting you like so much, Avery."

The girl's eyes grew wide. "Daddy, can we?"

Alex paused, appearing reluctant. Morgan wondered what his objection might be.

"It will be late, Sugar, when the program ends. We don't want to impose on Miss Morgan."

Morgan hid a grin at Avery's wounded expression.

"*Are* we an imposition, Miss Morgan?"

"No, never you. Your father, on the other hand," she teased, "he might be."

Confusion swept across Avery's face. "Daddy, whatever you're doing to impose, stop it. I love Miss Morgan's brownies, and I think I deserve a reward after the day I've had."

Morgan stifled a chuckle at the very adult-sounding girl.

Alex let out a burst of laugher. "Sugar pie, it's seems like it's been a long day for all of us. Miss Morgan, we'd be honored to take dessert with you in your home after the recital."

While they finished dinner, Morgan soaked up the feeling of comfort Alex and Avery brought. For a moment, they were like a family. Morgan's heartbeat settled into a warm comfortable rhythm, something she could grow to enjoy. When the tinkling sound of a little boy's laughter drew her attention, it was as though he was in the room, and she glanced around fully expecting to see her son. Instead, her gaze landed on the glowing angelic face of an eight-year-old girl.

"I really like this." Avery spooned up a large shrimp and slipped it into her mouth.

"Shrimp?" her father asked.

"Well, that, too. I like the three of us. Dinner at the table. Not Chinese food from a white carton on a tray in the family room."

Morgan's heart melted at the expression of satisfaction on the girl's face. Turning in Alex's direction, Morgan caught him nodding. His brown eyes lit with delight and locked on hers. He winked. "I agree."

Heat rose into her cheeks. Flustered, she didn't know how to respond.

Alexander Blake was definitely flirting with her.

Chapter Four

"Bye, Sugar." Alex waved to Avery before leaving her in the care of her choirmaster backstage at the school's auditorium.

He wound his way to the front to find Emma. She waved, and he headed to where she and her husband sat.

"Hi. Thanks for the seat, but if you don't mind, I'm going to sit with Morgan Marshall."

Emma smiled so wide, he thought it had to hurt her face. He'd bet big money she'd be texting his mother about this development before he could take a seat.

"You go right ahead." Emma shooed him away with a flick of her wrists.

Leaving his friends, he sought out Morgan. The cooking teacher, cookbook author, and television host most definitely captivated his attention. Dinner was an enlightening affair. The reality of her far exceeded the daydreaming he'd done in the past. Something about her drew him. Like a magnet to steel, he couldn't resist.

He didn't know what she'd said to his only child to quiet her and put a smile on her face, but she worked magic. Morgan represented what he considered wholesome and genuine in a woman. He couldn't call her the girl-next-door type because she clearly wasn't a girl, yet she held the same appeal. Morgan Marshall was a woman to be trusted. Someone he was very interested in spending time with alone. But for an unknown reason, he sensed her unease whenever he directed his full attention at her. He'd been disappointed when she refused to ride with him and Avery, instead choosing to take her own car and meet them at the recital.

"Hello, Tom. Susan." He spoke to the parents of Avery's schoolmates, nodded to several more. He stopped and scanned the large room decorated in swags of red and green velvet hanging from the rafters, searching her out—her dark brown hair that hung in soft curls at her shoulders. She had gone off to secure seats while he escorted his daughter to the appointed spot backstage as instructed.

"Morgan, where are you?" He didn't expect her to have ESP or to even hear him, but saying her name helped him focus on the sea of people.

When Morgan stood and waved, he spotted her and waved back. Making his way through the crowd, he couldn't imagine better company for the evening. He wasn't even sorry his parents were out of town. And, he realized, he was smiling. Genuinely smiling.

"Excuse me." He bumped the knee of an older woman as he made his way down the aisle to his seat. He repeated his plea to each person he passed. Morgan had picked prime seats.

They lined up with the center of the stage, ten rows back in row J. Was that coincidental? J stood for joy. Something that vibrated in him for the first time since… he and Avery had buried Casey.

"Thanks," he said, sliding into the seat next to Morgan.

"She's calm now, right?"

"Smiling like there had never been a meltdown."

"Good." The smile that played on her lips made him smile again, too.

After a deep sigh, his tensions of the day melted away, and he relaxed. He started to stretch out his arms, but then stopped. He wouldn't want her to think he was making a play for her with some sort of high-school move—the awkward arm stretch around the girl. He turned slightly in his seat and tilted his head closer to hers. "Are you going to share with me what caused Avery's tears today?"

Looking straight ahead, she smiled, and he watched her smile form easily on her lips.

She shook her head. "No. Not now. It was special girl talk. We can discuss it parent-to-parent later."

Alex turned when someone from behind tapped his shoulder. "Yes?"

"You two are the cutest couple. So you have a daughter in the program tonight?" a silver-haired lady, draped in strands of pearls, asked. "I'll bet she's beautiful, looking at the two of you."

"We—" Morgan began.

"Thank you." Alex interrupted, cutting her off. "Avery Blake is her name. She has a solo. It's listed in the program." He smiled brightly at the lady and then turned his gaze back to Morgan. She appeared surprised but didn't contradict him.

28

He figured the lady didn't need to know the intimate details of their life. It was enough that she considered them a couple. If others could see it, would it be possible for Morgan to see it, too? It wasn't until that moment he understood how much he truly missed being a family of three and having a wife, after being forced to let go of the woman he loved. It proved tougher than he imagined. Now eighteen months later, he looked forward to a new chapter of his life. Maybe one with Morgan Marshall playing a major role.

The houselights of the auditorium dimmed. A hush fell over the audience. The school's choirmaster appeared under a spotlight. "Good evening, ladies and gentlemen. Friends and family. Tonight, Savannah's all-girl Preparatory Academy presents its annual holiday show. Each year, we feature a solo artist from each grade level. It could be a singer or a musician. These students, singled out for this honor, have shown marked improvement over the course of a year and exemplify the kind of tenacity we seek to nurture at the academy. After all, talent without tenacity does not take them anywhere. Without further ado, I give you the Preparatory Academy choir and band."

Deafening applause rang out as the curtain rose to reveal the stage. All the kids he'd seen running around backstage were now garbed in white robes. The only thing missing—their halos. Alex settled in his seat and rested one hand on his leg. His hand brushed Morgan's. Instantly, they looked at each other. He patted her hand before she folded hers together in her lap. If the lights hadn't been so dim, he'd swear she blushed. Yes, indeed, Miss Morgan charmed him more and more.

With rapt attention, he took in each performance. It was too hard to choose which age group he enjoyed more. The sweetness of the voices of the younger children or the delicate harmony of the older students. The musical solos—one on the piano, another on a violin, and the last one a flute—convinced him the decision he and Casey had made to send Avery to the academy had been the right one for her. She thrived with the smaller class size, and she received special attention for her dyslexia.

Three quarters into the program, Avery moved from her spot in the choir lineup on the risers to take center stage. The choirmaster lowered the microphone to suit Avery's height. His adorable daughter began her first note a cappella. She projected her voice and hit a high note, a note he hadn't known she could sing. The auditorium filled with applause as his daughter continued her solo, the choir backing her up.

When Avery finished her selection and began to take her place with the others, the lady in pearls behind Alex tapped him on the shoulder again. "You and your wife must be so proud," she whispered. "What an angelic voice."

Alex watched as Morgan smiled and nodded, her face damp. With all the restraint he could muster, he kept his hands to himself, though he wanted to gently wipe away her tears and fold her into his arms for a comforting hug.

The program ended about fifteen minutes later with the performers receiving a standing ovation. As the houselights rose, so did Morgan. "I'm going to scoot out. I'll get dessert ready. Avery did a fantastic job. I know you must be so proud of her."

"She really moved you with her singing, didn't she?"

Morgan nodded again. There was something sweetly vulnerable about her. A slight tremble of her bottom lip. The way she cast her glance away. He wanted to hug her and reassure her that everything would be okay. But given her stance, he couldn't bring himself to cross the short distance. As she turned and left him, something told him to be patient, to wait for her to say something more. He offered a silent prayer. "Lord, if she's the one, and I think she is, you have to give me a clear sign, even if it takes a bump on the head."

After she departed, he stared at the stage, curtain closed, while people around him swarmed for the exit doors. Watching for a sign, he half expected the curtains to part and an angel to sing out *Hallelujah*, which in his mind would be the perfect notes. But he was far from perfect. If he received a perfect sign from Heaven above, it just might bowl him over dead.

That wouldn't do at all. Because then he would miss the pleasure of getting to know the lovely Morgan Marshall better.

He paused to focus on her in his mind's eye. "I wonder what her favorite flavor of ice cream might be." He truly wanted to know everything about her. But would she want the same?

Chapter Five

Morgan's hand trembled. She squeezed the steering wheel tighter to stop the tremors.

"Get a grip." Then she laughed at her own pun.

Traveling the most direct route home, she hurried, running a yellow light. A turning car honked and startled her back to reality. Nervousness had taken hold mixed with sweetness—she adored Avery and she really liked Alex. However, apprehension bubbled inside her. She recalled her darling in-laws' encouragement about dating again, but until the last six months, the thought was out of the question. Their accusation about her staring at a closed door way too long made her ponder their observations of her.

They insisted when one door closed, another opened—at the right time—but if she wasn't looking, she'd miss it. Though she appreciated their loving concern, she thought they had been too cavalier in putting the past behind them. Her time of grieving had taken much longer than theirs, maybe because they had each other. When Bryce and Justin died in the car accident, she had no one of her own. A few cousins scattered here and there, but no immediate family. Her therapist assured her she was doing just fine. To take her time.

But this year when summer turned to fall, she had a new spring in her step. The color of light made things around her glow in a new way. The sense of life surrounding her brought a renewal to her aching soul. At Labor Day, for the first time in a couple of years, she had an inkling from a vivid dream that Christmas would deliver a miracle to her. To her. Of all the people on the planet, she would be blessed with a miracle. Yet, that knowing deep in her soul made her flinch and look away. Why would she be more deserving than someone else? Her needs were small compared to so many others. Could she trust the feeling? Or was she no better than a doubting Thomas?

Maybe having an interest in a man is a miracle.

She liked Alexander Blake. He was kind. Something about him gave her confidence that in a crisis, he would seek to do the right thing, and at the same time, he would be strong, a strong arm of support. And she would be remiss in admitting she liked the way his eyes twinkled when he teased and the curl of his mouth when he smiled. Yes, the man was quite good-looking.

Was the tingling vibrating deep in her gut a sign that a doorbell was ringing, and she needed to answer it?

Was Alex interested in her as a woman?

Or mostly for Avery's sake?

Could she even hope to fall in love with the same depth and commitment she'd experienced with Bryce?

"Angels in Heaven, I need a sign. If I'm supposed to open

my heart and give a relationship a try, is it supposed to be with Alex? I like him. I'm interested." If only the curtain covering the auditorium's stage had opened before she left and a winged angel had sung out *Hallelujah*, then she could trust her instincts. But that hadn't happened. She intended to keep her eyes peeled for a signal. Hope was growing in her heart.

After pressing the button to turn on the car stereo, she turned up the volume on the classical station. A baritone sang deeply with great range and projection. Shivers raced through Morgan when the choir sang the chorus to *Hallelujah*. Her body relaxed fully for the first time in years. The music hypnotized. A deep contentment filled her. Gratitude swept through her. But the comfort she experienced—scary. She couldn't stay in that space for long after being emotionally shut away for a long period of time.

"Okay, so it's Christmastime," she argued aloud. "This song is to be expected. I need a real sign. A true sign," she pleaded as she pulled into her garage. After closing the door behind the car, she exited and started into the house. The tinkle of a little boy's laughter tickled her ear. She paused to hear more, but it had drifted away as though trade winds had swept it along. Instead, silence loomed loudly.

She washed her hands and went to the pantry, pulling ingredients for the brownies and setting them on the kitchen island. She turned on the oven to preheat, and then she gathered eggs and cream cheese from the fridge.

The brownies were in the oven when Morgan pulled plates from a cabinet and spoons from the drawer. She wished she'd already unpacked the rest of the Christmas decoration boxes. The pretty, red cloth napkins would go nicely with the cream-colored china plates trimmed with green holly, red berries, and rimmed with gold. They had been a gift handed down from her grandmother, to her mother, to her when she married Bryce. It would be comforting to use them again.

"Hot cocoa. I promised Avery." She crossed the kitchen to the fridge when the doorbell rang. It had to be them. She smiled. For a second, the image of them as a family sitting around the kitchen at night, all cozy and close, gave her heart a big shot of joy.

She turned on Christmas music and then opened the door. "Hello. Welcome."

Alex and Avery stepped inside.

"Your light is out." Avery pointed to the darkened porch.

"Thank you for letting me know." She hugged the girl. "You were beyond wonderful tonight. I enjoyed the program very much."

Avery blushed and cast her eyes down. "Thank you," she whispered.

"Let's celebrate," Morgan told her, lifting her little chin. "You know where the kitchen is. Brownies are in the oven. Why don't you wash your hands? I still have to make the cocoa. Would you get the milk out?"

"Sure!" Avery scampered off.

"You probably don't come in and out this way much." Alex pointed back to the porch before closing the door. "If you have a bulb and a stepstool, I'll be happy to change the light for you."

"I appreciate your offer." It was nice to have him ask. A very gentlemanly thing. However, she didn't need a protector or a handyman. She was quite capable of changing a light bulb. "Thank you, however, I'll take care of it tomorrow when it's light outside."

His forehead crinkled. "You would deny me the privilege of doing something nice for you…while you treat Avery and me?" He leaned in close. She stood very still, half wanting him to kiss her and half afraid he would. "I'm not that good in the kitchen. You and Avery could have some girl time. Her grandmother's been gone all week, and I think she really misses talking with her about girl stuff. It's only a light bulb, however, my thank-you for your rushing over to handle the meltdown earlier. I don't know what I'll do when she reaches those teenage years."

Morgan laughed. "Okay. I'll get the stool and light bulb, but let me put the milk on the stove first." She crooked her finger. "Follow me. I even have a tool belt, if it will make you feel more official."

"You have a tool belt?" He was only a step behind her. She chuckled at the curiosity in his voice. She enjoyed surprising him.

"It is the twenty-first century. Do I need to teach Avery how to use a hammer and a screwdriver?" She entered the kitchen where Avery sat on a stool at the island with the carton of milk in front of her.

"Daddy has prepared me," Avery said.

"Alex, I don't know what you're worried about. You're raising a daughter to cook and wield tools. That's quite an accomplishment."

"Yeah, but he's really glad you're teaching me about cooking." Avery nodded. "I think he's waiting for me to get older and learn more so I can cook for us more often."

"Then you've come to the right place. I promise you'll be on your way to being a chef if you stick with me."

Walking into a small closet off the kitchen, Morgan

reached for a bulb in the box where she stored extras. On her way out, she hoisted the two-step stool. "Here." She held the items up for Alex. "Make sure the switch by the door is off. Safety first."

When Alex headed out of the kitchen, Morgan turned to Avery. "Why don't you get the large measuring cup? Pour four cups of milk into that pan." She pointed to the one already on the stove. "I'll get the cocoa."

Morgan glanced at Avery to keep an eye on her, but she allowed her to handle the task without helicoptering. The worst that could happen would be spilled milk, which in the scope of life was nothing more than a ten-minute cleanup.

She secured the cocoa and held up the package for Avery to see. "Would you get a scoop from the drawer?"

Turning on the gas, Morgan began whisking the milk in a circle, making it swirl. "Now add the cocoa," she instructed Avery just as the timer for the oven dinged, a reminder to remove the brownies.

"YOW!"

The holler came from Alex. A clatter followed. A thud hit against the front door.

Morgan turned off the stove and pressed the timer button to cease the buzzing. She and Avery raced to the front door. When she opened it, the stepstool toppled over inside, clattering against the wooden floor.

"Owww," Alex moaned.

"Goodness. What happened?" Morgan searched in the dark to locate Alex. A moan came from below. He lay on the ground, three feet below, beside the brick porch. He was almost sitting, his head against the house, holding his shin. In five steps, she reached him, searching for signs of blood.

"Did you hit your head?" Did he have a concussion? "I think I need to call an ambulance."

"Daddy?" Avery wailed. "Daddy, please be okay." She began to cry. "Please don't let them take him away in an ambulance."

"Shhh, Sugar," Alex said hoarsely. He tried to push himself up but melted back against the house. "Avery, Daddy is okay."

"Alex, I really think I should call an ambulance," Morgan insisted. In the dim light, he shook his head.

"The worst of this is a sprained ankle. Could you help me up?"

Squatting beside him, Morgan reached an arm around his back. As she stood, Alex grabbed the porch for stability. She leaned him in that direction, fearing his injured ankle wouldn't be able to support his weight.

Avery, tears trickling down her face, hugged him from behind. "Daddy, you're okay?"

"Yes, Sugar, I am."

Morgan worried he might pass out given the pain flashing on his face. "Avery, go get my purse in the living room. In the kitchen closet, grab the broom." Like it or not, Alex Blake was going to see a doctor.

"No ambulance. No doctors. Too scary for Avery," Alex whispered in short bursts.

"We'll see." Morgan couldn't risk Alex being seriously injured.

Avery returned with the requested items in tow. "Here."

"Alex, use the broom for stability. I'll get my car."

A minute later, she drove her SUV across her manicured lawn. The closer she could get the vehicle to Alex, the easier it would be to get him inside with the least amount of pain. Or so she hoped.

"Avery, please grab the throw from my couch." Avery raced away.

"Alex, let's get you to the ER."

With Avery buckled in the back and Alex in the front passenger seat, reclined as far as it would go, Morgan backed out of her yard and onto the street. The nearest hospital was only a handful of minutes away. But going there was a path she dreaded. It dredged up memories of the evening she raced there hoping to hold her child before he took his last breath. Over time, the sharp pain of the memory turned to a dull ache, but the same urgency she felt then pushed her to get to the ER now as fast as possible.

In the backseat, Avery whimpered, "Momma. Momma. Momma."

Morgan's heart broke. Obviously, Avery connected the hospital with her mother's passing. If there were any other way, Morgan would've spared Avery the pain of this experience, but with Alex's parents out of town, she had no one to call upon to care for Avery this late at night.

After pulling up to the emergency room entrance, she got out and opened the door for Avery. "Honey Bear, I want you to walk in there very calmly and tell someone at the desk that your daddy hurt his leg and needs a wheelchair. Can you do that? Very calm and very grown up."

Avery's bottom lip quivered. She nodded. With her fists by her side, she marched rigidly to the sliding doors that *whooshed* open for her. Morgan closed the car door and went around to the passenger's side. "Alex," she whispered. "We're at the ER. Going to get you help."

He nodded, though his eyes remained closed.

"What's going on?" A man in scrubs jogged out the door. Avery, Morgan noticed, wasn't with him.

"Where's Avery?"

"Little girl is being taken care of inside. What happened?"

"He fell off a stepstool. Hit his head, maybe his back. He can't put weight on his foot, or maybe it's his ankle."

Alex nodded slightly. "She's correct."

"Be right back." The man jogged back inside. A second later, he rolled out a wheelchair and assisted Alex into it.

"I'll move my car and be right inside," Morgan called to Alex. She gripped the steering wheel to stop her hands from trembling, this time for a completely different reason than she had only hours ago.

"What if his injuries are worse than I think?"

Chapter Six

Wearing a gown in place of his shirt, Alex sat on the gurney in the ER examining room and waited for his turn for x-rays. The nurse had checked him out for signs of a brain injury, palpated his back to get a sense of the injury there, and then cleaned up the scrapes. Luckily, he hadn't sustained a concussion, but his head sported a goose egg of a bump, and a headache throbbed like a flashing red light in Savannah's harbor, reminding him there was something inside his skull.

"Does this hurt?" The nurse manhandled his leg.

"No. Of course not." He winced, refusing to cry out in pain, but if he had superpowers, she would've been vaporized.

"X-rays in just a minute." She turned and left the room.

He stared a hole in her back when no one was looking. The intensity of the pain had subsided a bit once the nurse stopped inflicting torture on him.

The doctor arrived a few minutes later and checked him

over again. The diagnosis so far: blow to the head without loss of consciousness, sprained back, and severe sprained ankle with possible fracture.

Alex added sprained manly pride to the accounting of injuries.

He hated hospitals. The sound of activity outside the door. The clock on the wall ticking loudly. The odor of cleaning supplies. Each minute had to be five in a hospital bed. He drummed his fingers and then stretched his hands. These folks could hurry the process along. Cast the foot. Send him on his way.

But…the injury was to his right foot. How would he drive? Shoving his fingers through his hair, he didn't know how he would handle things until his parents returned. Telling them was out of the question. They'd cut their trip short. He'd call Emma in the morning and have her help him make arrangements. Like a driver to take Avery to and from school. Someone to cook meals. Then there was the laundry to deal with.

Of all the times he could've picked to have an accident, this was the worst.

And his poor baby—although Avery would object to that moniker since she was eight, sometimes going on sixteen—suffered tonight. At one point, he considered asking the doctor to prescribe a med for her anxiety, but thankfully Morgan stepped in, took control, and distracted Avery in a unique way—teaching her about the machines and medical terminology. She showed her how to check a heartbeat rate and explained about blood pressure. The nurse was kind enough to allow Avery to listen to his heart with a stethoscope, which calmed her down significantly. Afterward, Morgan carted her off for hot cocoa.

When they returned, his heart surged with a rush of happiness.

He wasn't falling for Morgan in a big way because she brought joy to his child—she would do that for any child in need. Her ability to bring out the best in others, to nurture when she'd suffered so much, showed the goodness of her heart. The generosity of her spirit. These characteristics made her truly beautiful to him. He was more than a bit infatuated, giving him a natural high that painkillers couldn't touch.

Since September, he'd noticed a change in her whenever he visited the station. When he asked Peter about her, his friend shrugged and explained how she rarely spoke of her private life. He couldn't say whether or not she'd dated since her husband's passing. But Peter had thrown out a challenge—invite her to the New Year's Eve bash, the fundraising benefit for the station. The worst that could happen—she would say, "No."

He hadn't found the nerve yet to ask her.

In the chair beside the bed, Morgan held his sleeping daughter and dozed. What a disaster. He made a fool of himself and imposed on Morgan. She had better things to do than play nursemaid to him and his daughter. Friday night in the ER. Not the best impression. His chances for a real date in the future were probably pretty slim.

He stared at Morgan, her mouth slightly parted and her expression relaxed and peaceful, so lovely. Her manicured hands appeared delicate as they held his daughter. And yet, those hands had great strength and gripped him tightly when she helped him to the SUV. Earlier in the day, he'd looked on as her hands tenderly cupped the face of his daughter. She worked feminine magic, soothing Avery's fears and tears. Now sensations pinged in his chest, like a sparkler on New Year's Eve, coming at a moment when he was able to gaze unabashedly at her, and she was unaware of her full effect on him. On his heart.

She was an angel.

"Mr. Blake," the nurse said, barging into the room, interrupting his thoughts, and turning on the bright lights. He flinched. "I'm taking you for x-rays now."

Avery rubbed her eyes, groaned, and squirmed in Morgan's arms. Rising and slipping his daughter into the chair, Morgan draped her jacket over the recliner like a tent and blocked the light from his daughter's face, and then she stood next to the bed.

"May we wait here?" Morgan whispered and pointed to Avery.

"That would be fine."

"I'll take good care of her," Morgan told him when he slipped from the bed into the wheelchair the nurse provided and then squeezed his shoulder.

The quiet of the ER struck him as the nurse wheeled him down the hall. He needed to get out more. Live again. What did he have to lose? Yes, he would definitely invite Morgan to the party. Nothing risked—nothing gained.

No patients waited ahead of him when he reached the designated room. The whole x-ray process took only a few minutes.

"Officially, I have to wait for the doctor's approval to release you." The nurse delivered him back to the examining room. Morgan put her finger to her lips and pointed to a sleeping Avery. "But, I have it on good authority, no ankle fracture," the nurse continued in a whisper.

Morgan nodded as she listened as though committing all details to memory.

"You have a severe sprain," the doctor said, walking into the room. "Crutches. No weight bearing for a couple of weeks, could be up to a month or more, depending on how quickly it heals. Keep icing it to reduce the swelling for several days. Follow up with your primary doctor for further care in a week. I expect you'll need PT." The doctor nodded as though everything was settled. He left as quickly as he came.

"PT? Why would I want to do that? It'll heal. I'll be fine." Alex shook his head. The idea of spending any more time than necessary dealing with the foot seemed unwarranted. He had a busy life, especially with the holidays only two weeks away. Of course, he'd be up and walking in a few days. Okay, a week at most. A bum ankle would hinder dancing with Morgan on New Year's Eve.

"You're released to go, Mr. Blake. Remember about the follow-up care."

"Thank you, nurse," Morgan inserted. "I'll make sure he follows up as needed."

"There's a bright side to this, you know," the nurse said.

"What's that?" he grumbled.

"You're going home to spend the holidays with your family. Not everyone who came through those doors tonight is so lucky."

Before him, Morgan paled. He worried she might faint. Was this the hospital where her son and husband were brought after their accident? If so, he could only imagine what she must be feeling, experiencing, and thinking. The nurse sure put him in his place. He had a lot to be grateful for, including the woman who'd given up her evening to help him and care for his daughter.

"He will do everything to the letter that he's supposed to." Morgan's clipped tone insisted. "I shall make sure of it."

"Someone will be by with crutches and a wheelchair to roll you out of here," the nurse said as she left the room.

"Really, Morgan, you've done enough. Just get me home," Alex told her.

"Home? Really, Alex? How are you going to navigate stairs? Get sheets and bedding? Let alone make up the couch to sleep on? Who will cook for you and Avery? Who will take care of her? Help her get ready for school? Cook dinner? And according to Avery, you have only a half bath downstairs. No, sir. I've made other arrangements for you."

"You what?" He was taken aback by the general standing at his bedside. Where had the mild-mannered Morgan gone?

"You can be stubborn all you want. If so, I'll leave you to fend for yourself, but at the very least, Avery stays with me. My house is a single story. I have two spare bedrooms. I'm on hiatus from work until mid-January."

"I can't impo—"

"Hush. This is not open for debate. You need help, and I'm available to give it."

Begrudgingly, Alex grinned. "Whether I like it or not, eh?"

"Yes." Her fists went to her hips. He never should have doubted her ability to persuade. After all, she dealt with some pretty tough customers regularly—a group of eight-year-olds.

"All I'll commit to is trying. There's lots to do before Christmas. My mother is expecting a fully decorated house."

"You can negotiate later, Alex. Right now, let's get you

out of here." She gently woke Avery. "Honey Bear, come with me. We'll get the car and pick up your daddy. Let's go home."

As Avery followed along in tow, her hand fitting together with Morgan's, he couldn't help but wonder if Morgan's words, "Let's go home," were a turn of phrase or a prophecy of better things to come.

"God bless us, one and all," he said under his breath and meant it.

Chapter Seven

As Morgan drove home, her mind swirled. She hadn't had overnight guests in nearly a year. Beds had to be made. Pillows retrieved from plastic bags high on a shelf in the hall closet. Did she have enough eggs for breakfast in the morning? There was probably a package of bacon in the freezer. She had to remember to take it out before she went to bed. Eggs, grits, biscuits, toast, and fruit. Or maybe Avery would prefer pancakes.

She would set a table for three.

The memory of another time when her table was set for three popped into her mind. She smiled, feeling the presence of Bryce and Justin gazing down on her, giving her a big thumbs-up for helping Alex and Avery.

"Morgan?"

"Huh?"

Alex pointed to the right. "I think that was your street."

"Oh?" Flustered, she blinked to focus her tired eyes on the street sign. Sure enough, she'd missed the turn. Alex must think her an idiot…a woman who can't find her way home.

Pulling into a driveway to turn around, in the illumination of the headlights, she glimpsed a couple standing at the back of a car kissing.

"Oh my. Sorry for the intrusion," she called to the couple whom she was certain heard none of her apology through her closed car windows. Her cheeks heated. Thankfully, Alex wouldn't be able to see her embarrassment in the dim light. "That happened to me once. Only it was my grandmother's porch light. I was seventeen." She'd never told anyone that. The only people who knew were her grandmother and the boy she'd been kissing. Both now passed. She married that boy a few years later. It had remained a sweet memory for her and Bryce. But now she was babbling about it to Alex.

"Lucky guy," Alex teased.

"Yes," she mused happily. "He was." A lightness filled her. The ability to talk about memories of Bryce with Alex seemed natural. Comfortable. "And I was a lucky girl."

"I'll just repeat myself. Lucky guy."

"Here we are." She pulled into her own driveway. "I'll unlock the door, and then I'll carry Avery inside. I'll come back and help you, so please sit tight."

"Take care of my baby, please. I can manage on my own with the crutches." Something about the tone of his voice made her believe he wasn't a man used to being unable to help.

After Morgan opened the rear passenger door, she unbuckled the seatbelt for a sleeping Avery. Scooping up an eight-year-old girl proved to be more of a weightlifting challenge than she anticipated, but she accomplished it without fully waking the sleeping child, and even better still, not injuring either of them as she ran the obstacle course inside her home. Avery had to weigh three times her regular weight. Morgan vowed to add weightlifting to her weekly workouts.

Once inside the bedroom that had been her son's, she gingerly placed the girl on the bed. Six months ago, the bedroom looked like a toy museum and the bed resembled a car. A thrift store bedroom-set find and then some elbow grease had transformed the room into a gender-neutral space, comfortable for nearly anyone. The color scheme was taupe and turquoise. She'd been proud of handling it all by herself.

She removed Avery's shoes, pulled up her sox, and then covered her before turning on the night-light. The door remained ajar as she backed out. Hopefully, Avery would sleep peacefully through the night.

Returning to assist Alex, she found him out of the car and navigating one slow step at a time with crutches.

"Tomorrow, we'll make a few adjustments to make things easier for you. I have a rolling desk chair you can use as sort of a wheelchair."

Still in the hospital gown, he sat on the couch in the living room while she made up the second guest room. Moving quickly, she wished for eight arms to make the task go quicker. The image of an octopus in a maid's uniform made her giggle.

She finished the task and then rolled her office chair to Alex. "Rather than risk you falling over tonight because of those metal legs"—she pointed to the crutches—"sit here. I'll roll you into the bedroom. You can hop over to the bed."

"Thank you." Exhaustion etched his face. His brown eyes had lost their earlier sheen. Her heart ached to see him so tired. It had to be tough, especially with his support team away. But she was committed to helping him. No matter how much he tried to refuse. There wasn't a man alive who handled being a patient well, let alone dealing with a daughter, only weeks from Christmas. He needed her, whether he believed it or not. And she needed them.

After rolling Alex into the bedroom, Morgan parked the chair next to the bed. He insisted on climbing into bed on his own.

"I put out three pillows. You might want one to prop your foot on and another beneath your knee, and of course, the last for sleeping." She sounded more like a mother hen than a friend. That wouldn't do at all.

"You're a godsend. I appreciate your help. Tomorrow, I'll get things situated so Avery and I won't impose on you more."

"In the morning, we'll have a new day and a new perspective. Once again, you're not an imposition. It would be fun to have you and Avery help with the decorating while you recover. You point, and I'll hang ornaments, something I haven't done in a few years."

"You don't decorate every year?" Alex lay back on the pillow and closed his eyes.

She paused and wondered how to explain without sounding maudlin. "I haven't celebrated the holidays in a while. This year, I'm excited to renew the tradition, and I can't think of two people I want to share it with more."

"I'm too tired to launch a campaign against Saint Morgan." He yawned.

"Good night, Alex."

After taking the brownies from the oven and putting them away, Morgan lay her head on her pillow in the darkness of her room, where she remained still and listened to the sounds of her house. The tinkling of a little boy's laughter caused her to strain to hear, hoping to hear more. She waited expectantly. Silence filled the room. Sighing, she drifted off to sleep, smiling at the image of dancing gingerbread men in a chorus line.

The next morning a knock at her door woke her. She blinked several times. Was she dreaming? Someone called her name. Bolting upright, she recalled her houseguests.

"Miss Morgan?" Avery's sweet voice penetrated Morgan's still sleepy brain.

"Come in." She yawned. For some reason, she'd slept better than she had in a long time.

The girl slowly opened the door. Her angelic face appeared around it. "Daddy's still asleep. I'm hungry."

"Of course, you are. I'll get dressed, and we can make breakfast together. How's that?"

"Miss Morgan," Avery said, inching closer to the bed. Her small hands began to knead the holly and ivy quilted cover on the bed. "Do you like me?"

Surprised, Morgan nodded. "Yes. In fact, I adore you." She patted the spot beside her and motioned for Avery to climb up. Fluffing a pillow, she placed it behind the girl's back for support.

"Can I talk to you about something?" Avery's downcast eyes were worrisome. Morgan ran her fingers along Avery's forehead, pushing the girl's hair from her face. "Anything. I promise whatever we talk about will be just between you and me."

"What about Daddy?"

"What about him?"

"You won't tell him what I tell you, will you?"

Concern sliced through Morgan. She would do anything for Avery, but if this child was in danger of any kind or something had happened, she couldn't keep serious information from Alex. Having been a parent, she would want to know important information, and she suspected Alex, as a devoted father, shared that expectation.

"Well…How about if you tell me what's on your mind? If I think your daddy needs to know, I'll tell you. Together, we'll find a way to tell him. I won't go behind your back. Is that fair?"

Avery crinkled her nose, and after a moment, nodded. "So…people think because kids are small, we don't hear some things." Avery rolled her eyes as though some adults were too stupid to live. "I've heard a few women talk to Daddy, give him their phone numbers or email addresses, but later I've seen them helping at school or at church, and they stop me and ask me things about Daddy."

"Such as?" She couldn't fathom where the girl was going, but she intended to stick with the logic of an eight-year-old.

"Silly things. Does he drink coffee with cream or sugar? Does he like steak or seafood? Does he date?"

"What do you tell them?" Morgan held her breath. She was afraid to hear the answer. As cute as the girl was, every child had a moment when just about anything could come blurting out. She steeled herself not to laugh.

"Usually, I shrug. Act like I don't know anything. But *I* know what's going on. Momma talked to me before she died. She told me one day Daddy would hopefully bring a new woman into our lives. Momma said I had to be patient and caring. To try to love that woman, too, especially if we became a family."

Sadness flooded Morgan's heart. Avery's mother had tried to prepare her child for a stepmother coming into her life. What a brave thing to do. And yet, so heartbreaking to endure.

"I think…" Avery looked up at Morgan with hopefulness shining on her face. "I should get a vote about making a family again."

"Oh, Avery. I can't imagine your daddy trying to add a woman to your family without talking with you about it." The Alex she'd gotten to know over the last few years was patient, thorough in his work, also considerate. And most caring to his only child.

"I asked Daddy about it. He said to find someone to bring into our family to love us like Momma did, he would have to date."

Morgan smiled and adjusted her pillow. Talking with Avery was like a roller-coaster ride. The girl had adults pegged. They didn't give children enough credit for knowing what was going on. The girl beside her was wiser than her years. Any woman would love to have Avery for a daughter.

Avery reached over and patted her hand. "Miss Morgan, would you date my daddy?"

Surprise ricocheted through Morgan. She tried to keep a neutral expression. Of all the things she anticipated, those words coming from Avery's mouth were unexpected. "Date? Ahhh…"

"That's what Daddy says he has to do to find a new person." Avery's words rushed out. "If we're going to add to our family."

"I see." How in the world did she explain adult relationships to an eight-year-old child? What words could she use to explain chemistry, attraction, compatibility, and most of all, committed love?

"If you date him, then those other women can't, right?"

Stunned, Morgan stared straight ahead. Her mind whirred trying to find the appropriate words. Little Avery had given this topic more than just a passing consideration.

"I truly believe it will solve all of our problems," Avery insisted.

Morgan swallowed. With an uncanny grasp of her father's situation, the eight-year-old beside her sounded more like a thirty-year-old. This was most definitely a discussion Alex needed to have with Avery. Just the two of them.

When Avery waved her hand in front of Morgan's face, she flinched and tried to think of a way to skirt the topic of Alex dating.

"Miss Morgan, I have only one question about this dating thing."

"Okay, Avery." Morgan's voice wavered. "I'll try to answer it."

Outside the door, a rumbling noise sounded, drawing closer to Morgan's open bedroom door and distracting her.

Morgan leaned down when Avery quickly motioned her closer.

"Miss Morgan, would you please tell me what happens on a date?" Avery whispered.

All sorts of images of lashed through her mind before Morgan could formulate an answer. Her thoughts were interrupted when Alex rolled into the opening of the doorway and smiled. "There you are. Good morning, ladies."

Avery beamed at her daddy.

Morgan pulled up the covers around her shoulders and chuckled. In a very short time, the father/daughter duo had captured her heart. They brought happiness to her life she hadn't expected. Joy was truly one of the miracles of the Christmas season. But how in the world did she explain dating to Avery and tell Alex his daughter was setting him up?

Chapter Eight

"I came to see who wants breakfast," Alex said, sitting in the doorway to Morgan's bedroom, aware of the fact that the hospital gown hung down over his pants and he looked more pathetic than manly. Not the image he wanted to impart to the lovely Morgan Marshall. "I think I can manage a frying pan, a spatula, and flipping eggs. I'll cook."

"No." Avery and Morgan said in unison. The two faced each other and shook their heads, and then giggled.

The intimacy of the scene before him was a bit unsettling. He hadn't seen a woman in bed since before his wife died, but he'd been married to her. However, Morgan's sunny smile allowed his momentary discomfort to slip away. It filled his heart with a warming joy to see his daughter smile.

"How are you feeling this morning?" Morgan asked.

Avery hopped down from the bed and hugged her daddy.

"I'm happy it wasn't worse. I rewrapped my ankle. I gotta say, it ain't lookin' pretty."

"No significant pain?"

"The pillows kept it propped up. I don't think I moved all night."

"Good to hear. Now, why don't you and Avery roll into the kitchen?" Morgan asked. "I'll change and meet you in there. Avery, you know where the things are to set the table. Please wash your hands and start with that."

"Okay, but Miss Morgan," Avery wailed. "I *still* need an answer to my question." Avery's eyebrows wiggled. Her head bobbed to the side, and her shoulder twitched. Alex rolled closer to his daughter. Was she having some weird spasm attack? A second later it stopped.

"Girlfriend, we'll talk later. I promise." Morgan held up her hand, pinky lifted. His daughter hooked her pinky through Morgan's, and they giggled about their shared secret.

Alex shook his head. This was one of those times when he needed a woman in his life to interpret the female mind for him. Maybe later, he could pull Morgan aside and ask her to explain what that was all about.

"Marching orders, young lady," Alex said. "Let's go." He used his good foot to push off against the floor and send the chair in reverse. Morgan needed some privacy before breakfast.

Rolling through the house, he decided the ever helpful General Morgan was right. Trying to survive a two-story house on crutches would be a nightmare. Maybe she would help him by making up the sofa bed in his downstairs office, but then, that left Avery upstairs at night all alone. If she needed him for any reason, climbing the stairs with crutches could result in a tragedy of errors. He imagined himself tumbling backwards, landing in a heap, crutches broken.

When Morgan arrived in the kitchen, Alex rolled over to her. "I found everything to make coffee. I hope you don't mind. I rummaged through your fridge and pantry. What I don't know is—how do you take your coffee?" On the kitchen island sat a small pottery bowl with green packets of natural sweetener and a tiny pitcher filled with cream.

"I took a guess," Alex said. "Cream and sugar."

He was glad to see delight spread across her face rather than a frown. With some coaching, the kitchen need not be off-limits to him, though his wife had mostly banned him from the room at their house. She claimed when he even walked through, it usually resulted in a mess, so the only meaningful time he spent in there was when he helped clean up. Since Casey's passing, his mother did most of the cooking—coming to his house a couple of times a week to prepare and store meals. In return, he had earned a Ph.D. in microwaving and hitting speed dial on the phone to call for pizza or Chinese.

"I got the bacon and eggs." Avery beamed. "I put the bacon on the sheet, just like you showed in cooking class. Daddy insisted on putting it in the oven. Please tell him I won't burn myself."

"She's quite good in the kitchen," Morgan said. "We do a fair amount of baking, so she knows her way around the oven. And she knows safety first."

Alex rolled to the table. He bumped his foot on one of the table legs. Turning away, he didn't want Avery and Morgan to witness his grimace. The searing pain in his ankle hurt more than he imagined. To distract himself from the throb, he drank coffee while Morgan and Avery finished making breakfast. They decided on pancakes. Alex mused—if he ever wanted Avery to get a part-time job, she'd do well in a diner, given all she'd learned from Morgan.

"Avery," Morgan said. "Please find the pancake recipe in that cookbook." She pointed to one on a stand at the end of the counter.

"If you read me the ingredients, I'll gather them." Avery stood at attention and saluted.

"Well, now…how about you take control? You did the bacon, right?"

"Yes, ma'am."

"You read the ingredients and the directions to me. We can conquer dyslexia with continued practice."

Alex held his breath, expecting his daughter to balk. Usually, she avoided reading and offered a thousand different reasons. He fully expected her to grow up to be an attorney, given her logical presentation skills. No one launched a better argument than his child. Once, she'd refused to eat if she had to read the instructions for boiling spaghetti.

Avery scrunched her face and pursed her lips at Morgan. He expected to hear an excuse.

"Okay," Avery said. "But you have to help me so it doesn't take forever. I'm hungry. I want to eat—this morning, not this afternoon."

Avery and Morgan made it through the ingredient list as the timer for the oven went off. Morgan retrieved the bacon and set it aside. Returning to the kitchen island, Morgan helped Avery read the directions, and to Avery's delight, Morgan played sous chef. Alex learned just how bossy and demanding his little angel could be.

"Miss Morgan, will you please put the bacon on the

table?" Avery asked.

Morgan nodded. "Yes, Chef. Good idea."

Yet, as Morgan played the helper role, she asked questions, and it was obvious to him, Morgan was boosting Avery's confidence.

His heart wanted to hug her as much or more than his arms.

"Shall we eat?" Avery flicked the corner of the napkin and placed it in her lap as though ready to dine at a five-star restaurant. "Daddy, please say grace, and then pass the syrup."

They chatted through breakfast with Avery recounting the behind-the-scenes details of last night's choir recital. Had it been only last night? How interesting that an emergency could bond two—well, in this case, three—people together so quickly. Quietly, he observed Morgan. By all accounts, she appeared genuinely happy to have them as company. But he feared their staying beyond breakfast could wear out their welcome.

"What were your plans for today?" Morgan turned and asked Alex.

"We were going to buy a live tree and set it up at home."

"A real tree? Really, Daddy? I love the smell."

Alex chuckled. "Well, your grandmother wasn't happy with the short artificial one I purchased last year."

"I have a suggestion," Morgan said. "I think you each could use a change of clothes. Why don't I drive you to your house where you can pack a few things? I'd like you to stay with me, until you"—she pointed to Alex—"are able to get around better. Or until the cavalry returns to rescue you. Whichever comes first."

"I don't know…"

"We could pick up a tree for you. Take it to your house and put it in water. It would be ready for you when you're able to decorate it," Morgan suggested. "In the meantime, we could come back here. I had planned to decorate today, too. You could help me."

"Please, Daddy. How will we eat if we don't stay here? Momma would be mad if you ordered pizza every night until Mimi and Pops came home. I need good nutrition." The angelic smile on his daughter's face reminded him that she could act as well as sing.

He hated whenever Avery invoked something about her mother. It made him feel less than a good father.

Morgan looked down and sucked on her bottom lip. Her shoulders shook a bit. Apparently, Miss Morgan considered the not-so-subtle guilt his finagling daughter applied humorous.

Avery's apt comment kicked a field goal through the center of the uprights for two extra points. Food was an important element in their life. At breakfast, he and Avery talked about what they looked forward to that day. Over dinner, they discussed all that had happened while they were apart, along with some current events. He wanted his child well-versed in the world around her.

Besides, his mother had always teased his wife with the old saying about the way to a man's heart was through his stomach. If he allowed Avery to cook for them at home, he'd have a nervous breakdown. If he tried to cook for them both, they could end up in the hospital with food poisoning. He'd eaten Morgan's food a time or two—and the woman could cook.

For a little while, it made sense to accept her generous

62

hospitality. Staying with her would provide more meaningful insights into the woman whose smile and glow attracted him, especially first thing in the morning.

Somehow, he would find a way to show his appreciation. But what would she think of his growing affection?

Chapter Nine

"Avery, will you wait on the bench in the foyer? I'll be ready in a minute. I need to get your dad a new toothbrush. After we get you both a change of clothes, we'll be ready to pick out a Christmas tree. I think people might worry if he shows up in a hospital gown."

"Men," Avery huffed and rolled her eyes. "Sometimes they take the longest time in the bathroom. When Daddy shaves, it takes him longer than me to get ready. At least, he's got pants on."

Morgan chuckled. "I see." She retrieved the item for Alex from a stash in the hall closet and offered it to him along with a small tube of fresh toothpaste.

"Do you think of everything? Are you related to that Martha woman? You're organized. You have a television show. And a string of cookbooks. Wow. When I say it aloud, I realize what a celebrity you are."

"Just brush your teeth, Mr. Blake."

Smiling, Morgan pointed Alex to the bathroom sink. The tasks of life were no longer ordinary when shared with people she cared about. A sweet affection tickled her heart and anchored there. She enjoyed Alex's teasing.

"I'll be finished in a minute. Would you mind getting those crutches? I can't exactly roll your chair out of the house."

"Meet you in the foyer with them."

Crossing the living room, Morgan sucked in a quick breath when Avery picked up the crystal bell from the display in the foyer. "Honey Bear, I would prefer you not handle the bells."

"Oh. Okay. This one is *so* pretty." Avery stood on her tiptoes to try to replace the crystal bell. *Clank.* It struck the side of the shelf. Fear raced down Morgan's spine. Had it cracked? It was the last one the store had. It couldn't be replaced before Christmas.

"Wait. Please let me," she said as calmly as she could when Avery started to try again.

"It was easier to take down." Avery examined the bell, turning it around in her hands, and then placed the crystal ornament gently in Morgan's outstretched one. "I don't think I broke it." Her tone was fearful.

"It's okay. Let me take a look." After a quick examination, Morgan set the bell back on its perch. "All good. No worries." She let out a sigh of relief. "I'll be happy to show you each of the bells. They're a very special collection."

Avery counted. "One. Two. Three…Nine bells."

"Each one has meaning."

"What's that one mean?" She pointed to the one Morgan

had replaced on the top shelf of the display.

Morgan paused. What words did she use to explain that the bell represented her return to the living? "That bell is new. I picked it up yesterday. It represents good friends in my life, like you and your dad."

"And this one?" Avery pointed to one etched with baby booties on the bottom shelf.

"My husband gave me that one the year our son was born."

"You had a son? Where is he?" The surprise in Avery's voice took her aback. "Did his daddy take him away? That happened with a girl at school."

"Avery," Alex said gently as he rolled into the foyer. "We don't pry into other people's lives."

The girl cast her eyes downward. "I'm sorry, Miss Morgan. I didn't mean to be impolite."

Morgan squatted beside the girl and lifted her chin. She wanted complete eye contact before explaining. There was no need to overwhelm the child with more information than necessary, yet at the same time, she wanted to be sure Avery understood what she was explaining.

"I like to talk about him. His name was Justin. In a way, his daddy did take him. It was three years ago." Morgan swallowed before continuing. "They were in a car accident. Another driver ran a red light and hit their car. They didn't survive the crash."

Avery's eyes grew large and round. "You mean the way my momma didn't survive at the hospital when she was sick? They're in Heaven?"

As Avery's eyes filled with tears, Alex reached over and put a hand on her shoulder and gave a little squeeze.

"Yes, Honey Bear, my guys are in Heaven." Morgan tried to smile.

"Oh. I'm very sorry for your loss." Avery sounded so grown-up. She wiped her eyes before any tears fell.

Morgan shifted her gaze to Alex and gave him a quizzical look.

He shrugged. "She heard it over and over when her mother died."

"Miss Morgan?" Avery took a step closer. Morgan opened her arms, and Avery fell into them. "Do you think my momma is sharing time with your husband and Justin like we're spending time with you?"

Morgan drew in a breath as the girl's words washed over her. "I don't know, darlin'." She pulled Avery tighter to her. "But it would make me so happy if they were."

For a minute more, Avery clung to her. Morgan soaked up the love that only a child's arms could offer. She continued stroking Avery's hair. It had been so long since she hugged a child so thoroughly. Usually, she offered her students a quick embrace; it pained her too much to hug in earnest since Justin had died. Until now.

Drawing back, Avery said, "That would make me happy, too. I wonder what Christmas is like in Heaven."

"I'm sure it's grand," Alex said. He stood from the chair and grabbed the crutches. "They're surely outdoing us. Let's go get a tree."

* * * * *

"Hopalong Cassidy couldn't do it faster." Alex hobbled on crutches up the front steps to his house. With a quick glance over his shoulder, he sighted Morgan. She followed closely, ready to catch him if he fell backward. It was a comforting thought, Morgan as his spotter. Though if he fell forward, he'd end up tackling his daughter and hurting her.

"Who's Hopalong?" Avery asked. She pulled the house key from her pocket and inserted it into the lock.

"A cowboy. My grandfather used to tell me stories about him."

"Who names their kid Hopalong?" Avery scrunched her nose and then pushed open the door. She disappeared from sight.

"Mrs. Cassidy?" Morgan suggested, barely loud enough for him to hear. So she had a dry sense of humor, after all. He liked that. Just wanted to see a bit more of it. For some reason, she seemed shyer around him than when they met for functions at the television station.

"Watch your step," Morgan warned as he crossed the threshold.

Did she intend her words to have a double meaning? Was his conscience throwing up a warning to him regarding his physical movement, or was the warning intended to caution him about rushing her into…romance?

Romance? Wow. Romance.

Well, there it was. The true intention of his heart. He wanted to win over Miss Morgan Marshall's heart. But he wasn't a fool. He would tread carefully.

Then maybe he'd have a chance.

Chapter Ten

The piney scent of Christmas surrounded Morgan like a familiar dream. Christmas carols played through speakers placed on poles throughout the tree lot, and she bobbed her head as she walked in tempo with the beat. Ahead, a fence displayed different types of tree lights. Children raced around and shouted, "I found one!" referring, of course, to the perfect Christmas tree specimen. The cool December afternoon was creating the perfect heartwarming memory.

Avery ran on ahead to scope out trees. So far, each one she had picked, Alex had nixed. Too tall. Too misshapen. Too round. Not round enough. He insisted on at least an eight-foot tree. She never imagined the man could be so picky about a cut evergreen for his living room. Ornaments and lights often covered imperfections, and actually she preferred a less-than-perfect tree, one that had character. But she had to admit, she appreciated his dedication to his ideal. He had tenacity and patience for the hunt.

"When we get back home, I mean, to my house," Morgan said, following Alex down a row created by Christmas trees already set up on stands, "I'll get a foot tub, and you'll soak that foot. The doctor didn't intend for you to be on crutches for half the day."

"Yes, nurse. After we find the perfect tree, I promise to be a good patient."

"But you're going to try *my* patience," she teased. This was the third tree lot they'd visited. Soon it would be time for lunch. At this rate, they wouldn't make it back to her house until dinnertime. She unbuttoned her jacket. During a day in Savannah, she could experience the temperatures of spring, summer, and fall on a winter's day. It zapped her energy, tiring her out. But she looked forward to another meal with three plates on the table.

"What to make for dinner?" she pondered.

"Food?" Alex called out. How was it he heard her muttering over all the activity going on around them? She'd have to remember he had eagle ears. But could he hear the quickening beat of her heart whenever he looked at her, his eyes dancing with a smiling intensity? It was as though he was trying to memorize every detail about her.

"Daddy, halt! I've looked at everything. I want *this* one." Avery pointed to a tree next to her.

"I love that one." Morgan stepped up for a closer look. A Fraser fir. Perfectly shaped. With enough branches for her to thin some out and use them for a wreath. She and Avery would create something special for the door. After rubbing needles between her fingers, she sniffed. The needles released a fragrant pine scent. The freshness of the tree was evident by the

70

sap on her fingers.

"Looks like it's unanimous. Three votes." Alex raised a crutch high in the air. "Over here, my good man." His voice deepened as though performing a theatrical role in a play. "We shall take *this* one. Wrap it up."

"Daddy, you're silly sometimes." Avery giggled. She began to do some hip-hop moves while singing, "Wrap it up. Wrap it up. We. Be. Treed."

"Why don't you two start the trek back to the car? You can direct the guy to the correct vehicle while I pay." She handed her keys to Avery.

Alex steadied himself and reached into his pants pocket and pulled out a handful of bills. "This should cover it." He handed her the money.

"I would like to treat you and Avery to the tree."

Alex shook his head. "Nope. Absolutely not. I'm paying for my tree."

"But you paid for mine. Let me do this for you."

Nodding, Alex said, "Your tree is a gift from me and Avery for all your kindness. Trust me, what you're doing for us is worth the price of all the trees in this lot."

"Fine. You win this round. But you're still soaking that foot tonight."

With Avery in tow, Alex headed toward the parking lot. Morgan looked on fondly at the father and daughter. A day on crutches helped him get his hop-along walk down. Morgan didn't worry about him falling backward, or worse, doing a parking lot nose-plant.

Morgan waved over one of the attendants.

"You've found what you were searching for?"

She paused before answering. The guy had no clue how

his words carried a double meaning. Later that evening, when she discussed dating with Avery as promised, she would share how much she looked forward to a date with her dad. She hoped it might lead to something more. "Yes, I think I have," she said softly, a smile playing on her lips.

"Ma'am?"

"Sorry. This tree, please. Wrap it and tie it to the top of the red SUV parked on the left in the parking lot. You'll find a guy on crutches if you need more directions."

"Will do. You pay over there."

With her wallet out, she stepped up next in line to check out.

"You've got a sweet family," a woman's voice said from behind.

"Pardon?" Morgan asked, turning halfway to see who spoke to her. A short, gray-haired lady with a round face, round glasses, and round cheeks when she smiled, nodded.

"I watched you with your husband and daughter. What a lovely family."

Morgan remembered hearing similar words last night. She followed Alex's example. "Thank you." She didn't feel the need to explain the extent of her relationship with the father and daughter duo. "They're pretty special people to me."

"That's so nice to hear. You have a Merry Christmas, dear." The lady left the line and wandered away.

"You, too," Morgan called out, but a choir singing *Hallelujah* drowned out her words.

When she finally reached her car, Alex was dozing in the passenger's seat while Avery, in the driver's seat, pretended to drive. Morgan chuckled. When she was growing up, her father taught her to drive their ski boat. Later, when she learned to drive a car, it was much harder and scarier. But she wouldn't tell Avery that. For now, the girl needed her own daydreams.

"Hi," she whispered. "The patient is napping?"

Avery nodded and hopped out of the car. Morgan opened the back door for her.

"Don't forget, Miss Morgan." Avery's brow furrowed.

"About?"

"You said you would talk to me about dating."

"I haven't forgotten. Once we're back at my house and we've had some lunch, we'll talk before decorating my tree. Deal?"

"Yup."

As Morgan started the SUV and put it in reverse, she wondered how she would've handled this same question with her son. As though on cue, the tinkling laughter of a little boy rang out.

"Avery, do you hear that?"

"What?"

"Little boy laughter."

"Oh, sure. I hear it a lot. I didn't know he was your son. I thought a nice ghost came with your old house."

"Out of the mouth of babes," Morgan said. Avery's surprising response made her smile. Justin was with her everywhere. A happy, laughing little boy. Now that Avery knew about Justin, it would be easier to talk about him with her.

Traffic was snarled at nearly every intersection. Had all of Savannah left home to shop? "Patience," she muttered. Everything will get done with perfect timing. All she needed was trust.

Two hours later, with chores completed—the tree on a

stand in water at Alex's house waiting to be decorated at another time, Alex's ankle iced, her tree up at her house waiting for decorations, and lunch finished—Morgan filled a foot tub with warm water and Epsom salt and set it before him on the kitchen floor. Alex rolled a little closer to it.

"Sit here and soak, Alex. I promised Avery private girl talk. I'm going to turn music on low. Is there something in particular you'd like to listen to?"

"What's your favorite musical genre?"

Morgan thought for a moment. "I love Christmas carols."

He shook his head. "What would you normally listen to?"

"Classical. Jazz. Blues."

Alex brightened. "Jazz. That we have in common. How about some smooth jazz? It will help me relax while you heap your foot torture upon me."

The soft strains of Chris Botti and his trumpet floated on the air as Morgan went to the living room and dropped onto the couch next to Avery. It was her favorite spot in the house, allowing a view of her manicured lawn through the front window and a view of the fireplace. A great spot to curl up and read. Meanwhile, the Christmas tree in the corner, waited to be decorated.

"Why do you call me Honey Bear?" Avery asked.

"Why?"

"Yeah. I mean yes."

"I don't know…you're a sweet cuddly girl?"

"My momma used to call me that." Taken aback, Morgan blinked. That was not the response she expected to hear. What were the odds of both women using the same nickname for Avery? Was it creepy or sweet?

To Morgan's delight, Avery leaned and rested against her

shoulder.

"I talked to Daddy about dating. He said I couldn't date until I was thirty—but I know he was just kidding. When I told him I was talking about him dating you, he said—"

"Wait." Morgan put her arm around Avery and cuddled her close. "I thought you wanted to know what dating was all about. I don't think I'm comfortable talking with you about me dating your dad."

"But it's only dinner. Movies. And a goodnight kiss."

"Is that what your daddy told you?"

"No. I called Bethany and asked her while I was upstairs packing my clothes this morning. She has an older sister, ten years older, who dates. So I asked her. You mean you won't go out on a date with Daddy?"

If ever she used the word *flummoxed*, which she didn't, this would be the time for it. "Maybe. I'm not saying yes. I'm not saying no." Dating Alex...the idea shot pops of excitement through her, spreading a warmth of bubbly emotions. He was fun. There could be enjoyable times. Picnics. Art exhibits. School events for Avery. And Christmas every year.

But as the kaleidoscope of images turned in her mind, a panicky sensation bloomed in her chest. It might be too big a risk. If she and Avery grew more attached and things didn't work out between her and Alex, Avery might suffer—she'd already lost her mother. Add that to losing Justin—even if Avery were resilient—*she* couldn't withstand the loss of another child she cared for deeply.

No. Dating Alex Blake was not a good idea at all. Better not to mess with temptation. Caution was the best move. Keep his friendship *and* keep Avery safely in her life.

"Daddy *said* sometimes dating is harder when one person

has a child. Is it harder because of me? I thought you liked me. Or is it because I remind you that your little boy is gone?"

The depth of the conversation and the turn it had taken slapped Morgan dead center into reality. Avery was her Honey Bear. She would protect her like a mother bear. She would never hurt Avery.

The idea of dating Alex could only be a sweet daydream.

"Will you *please* tell me what dating means? It's not what Bethany's sister said?"

"Well... A date is when two people share a common interest and they spend time together to learn more about each other. Dating is when the two people like each other enough to have several dates."

"Then you get married?"

Morgan sat up straight, forcing Avery to straighten, too. "What? No... not necessarily. Sometimes when people date, they discover they don't like each other as much as they thought they might."

"That sounds like a guessing game or like a scavenger hunt."

Morgan chuckled. "Actually, I think you've discovered the secret to dating—for most people, it's some kind of game. Or maybe a test of sorts."

"Well, that's okay. Daddy is good at tests. I think I need to give him a chance. He said he only needed two dates to know it all."

Stunned, Morgan looked down at the girl. She pushed Avery's hair from her forehead and planted a kiss there. "Your daddy is a smart man. I don't know if I'm smart enough for him. No games. No tests. Not with me."

Two dates? Two dates? That's all he needed with her? To

then do what? Break things off before they got serious? Too late for that. Her heart was already on the hook.

It was time to plant her feet in reality. She and Alex Blake would not be a couple, no matter how cute others thought they looked together. It pained her to be excluded from the gift of raising Avery, beyond teaching her cooking and maybe attending future recitals. But that was that. Her mind was made up...though her pounding heart was protesting loudly.

Trying to maintain composure, Morgan crossed one leg over the opposite knee. No need for a couple of pity dates with Alex. If he asked her out on an official date now, she would turn him down.

Friends. That had to be enough of a relationship. Now and forever.

She just hoped she didn't dream about him when she closed her eyes at night.

Chapter Eleven

Alex rolled to the kitchen door as Morgan prepared to leave for the grocery store. "I insist on paying for groceries." Her mood had changed, and he couldn't discern why. After she left, he'd talk with Avery to see if his daughter's chat with their hostess revealed any insights. If luck smiled on him, after dinner, he would have a chance to take a romantic stand and invite Morgan to the New Year's Eve bash. But would she want to be seen with a guy in a wheelchair? Dancing with a chair couldn't possibly be as endearing as it was made out to be on television and in movies.

"Alex, when I want your money, I'll ask for it. I'm trying to do a nice thing here. Please just accept my friendship." Morgan bolted out the door.

"Wait," Avery called. "I want to go with you."

Alex grabbed his daughter's arm as she raced through the kitchen. "Sugar, let her go alone. I fear we're overwhelming

Miss Morgan."

Tears welled in Avery's eyes. "But Daddy, I wanted to go. Momma used to take me."

Was his child trying to replace her mother with Morgan? Trying to find a place of comfort? It broke his heart to watch tears slide down her face.

"Sometimes, the holidays can be…difficult for people. Like it was for us last year, after Momma went away."

Avery stomped her foot. "Stop it, Daddy! Momma died. D. I. E. D. I know about dying. People go to Heaven and never come back. At least, Miss Morgan has Justin. He comes and laughs with her. Momma has never come back for me!" Sobbing, Avery ran from the room.

"Oh, crap." Alex shoved his fingers through his hair. Grief was such a tricky bugger. Maybe staying with Morgan was a bad idea. For her *and* for Avery. His sweet girl needed to fill the hole in her heart left raw by her mother's death…and it looked like she wanted Morgan for that. Morgan had her own grief to deal with, and holidays, he'd read, were often most difficult for those who'd suffered the loss of a loved one.

But what did Morgan want? Need?

Alex rolled to the guest room where Avery lay face down on the bed and sobbed into a pillow. Had he pushed Avery and Morgan too far? The fall was an accident, but he'd used it to get to know Morgan better. Too much, too soon?

Stroking his child's hair, he said, "Sugar, are you okay? You need to catch a breath."

"Go. A…a…way!"

"I can't do that. I'm here for you."

Avery's sobs slowed. He continued to stroke her hair. Patience, he'd learned, was as much an art as a virtue. After a few minutes when Avery turned on her side and moved out of his reach, he offered a few tissues. She snatched them from him.

Alex sighed. "Did I do something wrong? Did I upset you or Morgan?"

"*You*!"

He'd gotten good at twenty questions with his daughter since Casey died. "I'm sorry. I apologize. I would never purposely hurt you or do something wrong. Could you please share with me what I did? Then, I'll try not to do it again." The family therapist he saw to help with Avery's grief and frustrations explained that he needed to always remain calm. Never raise his voice. And try to get Avery to verbalize her feelings.

She sniffed and blew her nose, then tossed the tissues at him. They landed on the floor. He didn't move to retrieve them. Instead, he handed her a few more.

He waited for her breathing to even. When no more tears fell, he tried again. "I love you. I want to help you. Please tell me what I did, so I can fix it."

"You can't."

"Well…sometimes I have talents beyond the obvious." Was he no longer her hero? The thought was crushing, but he was unwilling to give up. "Okay, maybe I can't. However, you might feel better if you talk about it."

Avery pointed at him. "It's *your* fault."

"Okay. It's my fault."

His daughter rolled close to him and stared him down. "You made Miss Morgan feel stupid."

Shaking his head, Alex stared at his crazed child. "Ah, how did I do that?"

"I don't know. I told her what Bethany's sister said about dating—dinner, movie, and a goodnight kiss. Then I told her what you said about tests. She told me that you were smarter than she was. You must have done something to make her feel that way."

"Sugar, I swear, I don't know what I did. But what if we talk with Miss Morgan when she returns?"

Avery sat up, scooted until her back rested against the headboard, and then she crossed her arms. Her bottom lip trembled. "Do you think Miss Morgan won't go out on a date with you because she doesn't want me around?"

"Oh, Avery." Alex hoisted himself on the bed and pulled his child into his arms. She let loose another flood of tears. He rocked her while she cried. "I don't think it has anything to do with you." He certainly hoped it didn't. Couldn't imagine a child being a barrier to any sort of relationship with Morgan. From all he had witnessed, she loved kids, and she was especially fond of his.

Stretching out on the bed, he lay beside his whimpering child, his heart breaking, and tried to offer comfort. He always worked to be careful with his words and explanations about life, but sometimes he was just a guy, never able to offer the tender nurturing support a mother could give.

A few minutes later, Avery's breath puffed from rounded Cupid's bow lips. She had fallen asleep. Closing his eyes, he wished for a time when grief and heartache were no longer land mines to navigate, that memories were sweet and cherished.

A bit later, he woke with a start. He must have fallen asleep, too. A sound startled him. Disoriented, he sat up carefully, not wanting to wake Avery. A second later, he recognized the room. Morgan's house.

As though poked with a grappling hook, Avery suddenly sat up and charged from the bed. "Morgan!" The scream was one of desperation.

Alex followed, hobbling on his injured foot.

Morgan was at the front door and turning around when Avery raced toward her, launching herself at Morgan. Horror seized Alex. He ran. His daughter's foot kicked the foyer table. Bells began to *clink* and topple.

Morgan caught Avery in her arms.

The bell stand rocked off the table onto the floor. Glass and crystal shattered everywhere.

"Ohhh!" Avery wailed.

Morgan stood statue still.

As Alex knelt to search for any unbroken bells, Avery broke from Morgan's embrace and raced out the front door.

"Wait!" he called after Avery. A piece of glass sliced his hand. Before he could do or say anything more, Morgan turned and followed after her.

"What a mess I've made of things." Making it to the kitchen, his foot throbbing, he grabbed a piece of paper towel and found his crutches. He offered a silent prayer that Morgan had found his child. And he offered another prayer of forgiveness for the misery they'd caused Morgan.

Her bell collection was irreplaceable. A sickening slosh roiled in his gut.

There was no way to make up the loss to her.

That knowledge could crush his very sensitive child.

"Avery?" he called as he walked through the front door. Heart-pounding fear tripped hard in his chest when he didn't spot her nearby. A list of disasters rolled at warp speed through his mind. What if she ran out in front of a car? What if she fell and was knocked unconscious? What if someone lured her away? "Avery," he shouted at the top of his lungs. "It's okay, Sugar. Come here!"

"Avery!" Morgan shouted a block down the street as she looked through bushes in her neighbors' yards. A woman came out to ask what she was doing. "I'm looking for a girl. She's very upset. She's only eight. Light brown hair and cute dimples. She was wearing jeans and a t-shirt, but no shoes or jacket."

"It will be dark soon," Alex called out. "Avery is my daughter. Would you help us search?"

Hobbling on the sidewalk, Alex continued to shout out messages, encouraging his daughter to appear. He wanted to scream and demand she show herself, not because he was mad, but because terror wracked his entire body. He couldn't lose his precious child.

Within twenty minutes, a half dozen of Morgan's neighbors joined the search.

Morgan raced up to him. "She couldn't have gone far. I'm going back to the house to check. If we don't find her in fifteen minutes, I think we need to call the police. I am sooo sorry about this, Alex."

"Oh, Morgan. It's all my fault. I'm sorry for all the problems we've caused you."

Shouts for Avery popped off every other second like an off-key calliope. Fear scratched its way up to Alex's throat. He swallowed against it and continued to search. "Where are you?" he begged.

Minutes ticked by. No Avery. His foot throbbed. His hip hurt. His back ached. But none of it compared to the raging fear in his chest. Where was his daughter?

Five minutes later, Morgan stood on the front porch of her house. "Alex!"

He turned to find her standing on the porch with the front door wide open. He raised a crutch to signal to her.

"Found her!" Morgan motioned to him to hurry.

The neighbors applauded.

As fast as his crutches allowed, Alex moved at a quick hop-along pace. Reaching the steps, he dropped the crutches and ran up to Morgan's door, the pain in his ankle tame compared to the pain in his heart.

Morgan greeted him, her expression troubled. "Go easy, Mister. She's quite upset still."

Inside, he spotted Avery on the couch. Hands folded. Head hung so low, he couldn't see her eyes. Between where he stood and where she sat, the foyer table had been removed. No trace of the bell stand. No broken glass.

With a hitch in his step, Alex crossed the room to his child. He knelt down on the floor in front of her and pulled her into his arms.

"I'm so sorry," Avery wailed between small gasps of air.

"You're all right?" Alex cupped her face, kissed her nose, and ran his hand along her arms. "Sugar, you scared me senseless."

"Daddy, I'm so sorry."

"Shhh." He hugged her, memorizing every inch of her. "Just don't ever do that again."

"I can't." Avery hiccupped.

"Okay… good to know."

Avery whimpered. "Can't replace the bells I broke."

Morgan appeared by their side. She bent and kneeled, too. "Avery, you're what's important to me." Morgan threw her arms around Avery and Alex. "Group hug."

They clung to each other. One of the neighbors came up on the porch and closed the front door. As Morgan hugged them tighter, Alex wondered if she was being nice, trying not to make a bad situation worse. If she was trying to protect Avery when, in fact, her heart was breaking over the loss of her treasures. The bells held significant memories of her beloved husband and son.

"I'm sorry for being so…stupid, Miss Morgan. I didn't mean to break your things. And Daddy, I'm sorry I ran away. Please don't hate me."

"Shhh. No, Sugar. I could never hate you."

"Avery, you're safe. Unharmed. That's all that matters to me," Morgan insisted. "And I never ever want to hear you call yourself—or anyone else—stupid."

In his arms, Avery finally relaxed a little bit. Alex noticed her feet, scratched and dirty. "It's been a long day. Avery and I should go. If it wouldn't be too much trouble, after all the damage we've done, would you take us home?"

Morgan shook her head. "You can't leave. You have to stay. I get my turn to tell the two of you how I'm feeling. But first, we need to take care of the injuries while I gather my thoughts."

Rocking back on her toes, she folded her arms over her chest and eyed him like a determined general, but compassion radiated from her gaze. Her eyes filled with tears.

Confused, his thoughts swirled like eddies in the Savannah River.

This was a side to Morgan he'd never seen.

Christmas Bells

Chapter Twelve

Morgan set the table for three. Paper napkins with poinsettias on them. Spoons. Forks. And knives. She hummed *Hark! The Herald Angels Sing* as she placed a mixed green salad on a small plate beside each large bowl and then slid a pot of grits to the center of the table. Hoisting a sauté pan, she placed it next to the pot. Shrimp and grits. A low-country favorite. Pouring sweet tea in each of three glasses, she stood back and surveyed the table. The meal might be their last together. If so, it had to be as positive a memory as possible. The events of the last twenty-four hours could crush a weaker person. Not Alex. And certainly not Avery. She hoped she could be as brave as they.

"Smells great." Alex rolled into the kitchen with Avery, fresh from a bath, dressed in reindeer pajamas.

"Hungry, Honey Bear?"

Avery nodded her head shyly. Morgan ruffled her hair.

"Let's sit down."

Once everyone was at the table, Avery said, "Could we hold hands and tell what we're grateful for?"

Alex raised a quizzical eyebrow at Morgan. She smiled. "I think that's a wonderful idea."

Avery stretched her arm across the table. Morgan reached for it. In her hands, she felt the heartbeats of two special people. She squeezed both their hands.

"I'll start," Avery said. "I'm very sorry for ruining your bell collection. Thank you for being kind to me."

"I'm thankful you're safe." Alex nodded at his daughter. "I'm very grateful we have a wonderful friend in Miss Morgan."

"I am very grateful we're together. I find family-style dinners very comforting."

"Amen," Avery said, smiling.

After each had finished the salad, Morgan pulled warm garlic bread from the oven. She served up grits in each bowl and then ladled the shrimp and broth over it.

"This is so good." Avery rubbed her tummy. "Will you teach us how to cook this in class someday?"

"I'd be happy to have you help me make it next time." Morgan took a bite and savored the flavors. She would forever remember this meal whenever she ate shrimp and grits.

"I want to keep things on a lighter note. I planned to slide this under the Christmas tree so it would be your first present." Alex nodded to Avery. She pushed her chair back and walked to her father's seat. From behind him, she lifted out a gold-foiled rectangular box.

"This is from us." Avery presented the gift.

Morgan's hand went to her chest. "For me? Really? Oh

my. I don't have presents for the two of you yet."

She stared at the box and chewed her bottom lip. "I have something I would like to say before I open this, if I may."

Her dinner guests nodded.

"I've been told by two other people whom I know love me well that I have stared too long at a closed door. In doing so, they feared I wouldn't see when a new one opened. So while the events of the last twenty-four hours have been somewhat strange and sometimes painful, I believe I've stumbled through a new door without even knowing it. Until now. Alex, I'm sorry you were hurt, but my front porch never attacked anyone before, so I didn't know to warn you. Avery, if I put a table in the foyer again, I'll be sure to either nail it down or glue it. What I'm trying to say is that while I grocery shopped alone and talked to the onions and celery that have given their life for this dinner, I found it's more meaningful to have a discussion with people. Not just any people, but the two of you. People I love."

Avery's mouth formed a small 'o'.

Avery quickly scooted from the table and threw her arms around Morgan. "I love you, too. We love you. Don't we, Daddy?"

Alex grinned. He reached for Morgan's hand, and he rubbed his fingers over the top of her hand. The slight friction warmed her hand and her heart. He winked. "Why don't you open your present now?"

Carefully lifting the lid so as not to damage the gold foil, she set it aside. In a bed of red velvet lay a silver bell with a polished wooden handle.

"It's lovely." Morgan lifted it from the box. A little shake and a beautiful tone emanated from the bell and filled the room.

"I've had it for a long time. Actually, since birth. My grandmother collected all sorts of bells. This was a gift to my mother when I was born."

"Oh, Alex, I can't accept this." It would be a family heirloom. Something he'd want to pass to Avery someday.

"Oh, Morgan. Yes, you can. I'm hoping you'll use it to summon us to dinner many times in the future."

The tinkling of little boy laughter caught her attention. Clearly, Justin approved.

Morgan shook the bell again. "Yes, I'm sure I can do that."

* * * * *

After dinner was cleared from the table, Morgan popped corn and set a big bowl on the coffee table in front of them. She joined Alex and Avery on the couch to watch a Christmas movie. "This is so relaxing." She sighed and dimmed the lights. From her spot, the soft light glinted off the silver bell she'd placed on the mantle.

Avery popped up and grabbed the bowl of popcorn and then nestled herself between Morgan and Alex.

"Now, here are the rules for this evening," Alex said to Avery. "After the movie, no excuses, you're off to bed. Just one movie. Agreed?"

Avery smiled wide. She shook her head three times.

Alex felt her forehead. "Are you okay? Where's my daughter?" He tickled her.

Avery giggled. "It's a date."

"What?" Alex and Morgan said in unison.

"It's just like Bethany's sister said. A dinner. A movie.

And a kiss goodnight. That's what we're doing. It's date night."

Morgan tried to hide a grin but gave up. She chuckled, and her body shook with joy.

"See, Daddy," Avery said with glee. "We're going to date Morgan."

"Well…" Whatever Alex intended to say, he never finished.

When the movie began to play, Morgan reached her hand into the bowl of popcorn and felt a warm palm as Alex grasped hers for a brief moment. On the television, a choir sang *Hallelujah*.

Thank you, she mouthed, looking heavenward. *Got the sign loud and clear*.

Looking over Avery's head at Alex, Morgan whispered, "This is the best date I've had in years. And it's good to know in advance that it will end with a kiss."

Alex nodded in agreement.

Morgan leaned down and kissed Avery's cheek. "Honey Bear, you need to learn to share the popcorn."

"God bless us, one and all," Avery said and reached for another handful of popcorn.

The End.

Linda hopes you will enjoy the first chapters of *Her Heart's Desire* and *Behind The Mask*.

Her Heart's Desire

LINDA JOYCE

"Emotional. Compelling. Only as Linda Joyce does." ~ LovExtra Magazine

Lia & Lucas ~ The Sunflower Series

Her Heart's Desire

By

Linda Joyce

Chapter 1

Lia grimaced.

"*You will fail.*" Her brother's words echoed in her mind as she marched to her truck. She needed to charge her brother rent for occupying space in her brain. But sometimes, she mused, strangling Craig might be easier. His words clanged in her head, causing a tug-of-war between remembering them and shutting them out.

Midstride, she tripped. The toe of her boot caught a stone at the edge of the driveway. Packages flew from her arms. She wobbled and managed to right herself, but boxes littered the concrete. Tormenting frustration scratched its way up to her throat. She swallowed hard, forcing back the choking sensation.

"Could today get any worse?" she shouted and looked up, expecting to find a dark cloud hovering over her head. Instead, September's clear blue sky stretched far and wide. Hummingbirds, thick like a herd of cows, flitted from one feeder to another along the fence line. Breezes carried a *neigh* from her neighbor's horse in the next pasture.

Out near the road, a cloud of dust rolled by. A battered blue pickup kicked up dirt. Once again, Lucas didn't bother to stop. She'd already failed with him.

The world continued around her, just another day in paradise, except for almost a year she'd only been chasing serenity that paradise promised. It was almost in her grasp, yet one misstep would ruin everything. She'd go down fighting to prove her brother wrong. She just refused to fail.

Lia collected the packages and stacked them neatly on the back seat of her Ford pickup. When she turned the key in the ignition, the diesel engine rumbled to a start. Putting the truck in gear, she sailed toward town with a sliver of renewed hope the day would somehow get better. It took some fight, but she vowed to remain a *glass is half-full* kind of girl.

Behind her truck, the two-lane farm road disappeared in a cloud of brown dust. Wearing her best cowboy boots, she let up on the gas just before the truck hit a pothole the size of a wagon wheel. She bounced hard as though on the back of a bull, so hard it rattled her teeth. She'd suffered many bumps in the last year, and as bad as they were, they hadn't crushed her yet. Almost didn't count.

She glanced behind to the boxes now scattered as though someone had pitched them like a deck of cards into the air and let them fall. The stuff in the boxes, on their way to new homes, was money in the bank. Money that kept her in groceries and gas, but never prevented life's next bump from crashing into her world. With a little serendipity—she didn't dare wish for the full-blown luck of the Irish, just a tad to help cover looming debts—she would manage to keep her farm for another year. One year at a time.

Pushing away all thoughts of Craig and future tomorrows, she recited her list of errands. "Drop off the outgoing mail at the post office. Pick mine up. Drive ten streets to the opposite side of town for Karl Turner."

Since she hadn't had more than a second date with any man in the last year, she set her sights on the new manager who'd moved down from Chicago and worked at his uncle's farm store. He thought she was coming in for a large order of tulip, daffodil, and crocus bulbs for fall planting.

"News flash! Lia Britton trolls for a date," she said aloud.

The information would shock every last person in Harvest, Kansas, given her family's position as upstanding pillars of the community, a family who dotted i's and crossed all t's. The Brittons were proper people, proper with a capital P.

For once, she wanted to get past the inquiry of first and second dates. "What's your favorite food? What's your favorite color?" Though several months ago, on a blind date, a man asked, "What brand of condom do you prefer?" Stunned, her sense of humor stalled, and she left before dessert.

Even a lowly artist and farm girl enjoyed a good meal and good conversation in the company of a good man. She was no exception. Would her dark denim skirt and off-the-shoulder, soft pink peasant blouse, something she'd discovered in one of the hundreds of unopened boxes in the barn, along with a bright smile prove country enough to catch Karl's eye? She'd worn the outfit hoping it would bring success to her mission.

She needed a date.

Besides, there was no reason he had to know why next Saturday night held such special significance. If she managed to land a rendezvous with him, it would give her something to look forward to...something to get her past the haunting pain of tomorrow.

Lia slowed, bumping the truck onto the fresh asphalt of Main Street and into the afternoon shadows cast by two-story buildings. She flicked a quick wave at Helen Carter standing in the window of the Sunflower Café, rolling by without slowing. Last week, the older woman had cornered her when she went in to order a birthday cake. Helen insisted on telling her fortune, which Lia hadn't wanted to know. Bad news was something she preferred to read in the paper rather than worry and wait for it to come true. Like sour milk, it could ruin a day...or a life. She'd had enough negative news to last a lifetime. But Helen, whose accuracy rate matched a master sharpshooter at a gun range, grabbed Lia's wrist when she offered her credit card to pay. Helen then proceeded to announce to coffee-klatch customers how Lia would soon have a man in her life. A man she already knew.

"Yeah, right," Lia mumbled, remembering the group's hearty applause and her own reddening embarrassment. An irritating flush heated her cheeks. There was only one man she wanted, but he'd rejected her, avoiding all entanglement except those resembling a brother-sister relationship. She had a brother. Didn't want another one.

She angled the pickup into an empty place in front of the post office. "A man in my life." She grunted. "As if men have been beating down my door."

Lia stepped onto the truck's running board, then hopped down, hoping to make a graceful exit in a skirt. With the first of three stacks of boxes in her arms, she carried them in for mailing.

"Afternoon, Lia," Zoë Marshall, Lia's friend since grade school, called out from behind the counter. "How many this time? Single-handedly you've kept this station in business for the last year."

"Don't know. More in the truck." Lia plopped the boxes on the counter. A delivery service would pick up at the farm, but that's how hundreds of boxes ended up there in the first place. A service would've been easier than hauling boxes to town each week, but she'd never see a living soul if she didn't make the weekly trek to the post office and to church. At the farm, corn listened well; however, other than rustling with the wind, it never talked back. Hard to have a conversation even though there were acres of ears and only one of her.

After Lia stacked the final load of packages on the counter, Zoë weighed each one, punched numbers into a machine, totaled the cost, and handed a receipt to Lia. "We need a girls' weekend away. Before the cold blows in, let's go to the Renaissance Fair in Lawrence."

"Sorry, you know I don't like costumes."

"Well, then, how about that blues club over in KC?"

"I love their barbecue, but don't like smelling like it."

"Why do you keep putting me off?" Zoë pouted.

"How about horseback riding? A neighbor will loan us a couple horses for an afternoon."

"Lia, we have to do something to get you off the farm." Zoë's tone chastised. "God knows it was awful what happened to your parents, but dang, girl, you didn't die with them."

Lia flinched. The painful rawness of her parents' death had healed, but a tender spot still remained. "I'm not the wild child I was when we were in high school. The old place is comforting. Makes me miss my parents less. Besides, you see me every week, sometimes twice with church."

"There's only so much to paint on the prairie. I thought surely you'd be ready to head back to the city after a few months." Zoë paused before whispering, "Of all of us, I thought you'd be the one to make it out for good."

She'd thought so, too. Except now, the rolling hills dotted

with farms surrounding Harvest offered her endless inspiration. The same field, or stream, or copse looked different with each season. A simple tree dropped leaves in winter. Sprouted fresh green in spring. Bloomed rich deep green in summer, then turned red, gold, and orange in the fall. Every season offered a colorful palette. The fields had character, too. A blue sky transformed at dusk, glowing pink, gold, and even lavender. The scent of fresh-cut hay was like the warm embrace of an old friend.

Sometimes she missed the city, missed her students more, but here she could breathe deep with the wide-open sky. Here, she vibrated with life as though the country had tapped her with a tuning fork and together they pulsed with the same frequency. It had taken leaving and returning for her to figure it out.

Zoë leaned over the counter and waved Lia closer.

"Are you mad at me because that cowboy at Rockets asked me out for Saturday night?" Zoë whispered.

Lia lowered her eyes and shook her head, trying hard not to laugh. Good-hearted Zoë, with her dark brown eyes expressing her every emotion, would be pleased to know she hoped to wrangle a date with the newest man in town, and the cowboy in question would never be her type.

"If you're interested, really interested, I'll let you have him."

"Oh, no, Zoë. I'm doing just fine. Are you mad at me because you don't have a place to crash in the city? Is that why you keep wanting me to leave?"

"No." Zoë drew back and placed a hand over her heart as though mortally wounded.

"But?" Lia whispered.

"The cowboy fits the description of the man Helen said

would come into your life." Zoë furrowed her brow. "I can't mess with fate, nor should you."

"You go on and have a great time with him tomorrow night. You know, this could be the time when Helen is wrong. No one's perfect."

Zoë gasped and shook her head as if to negate Lia's uttered blasphemy.

Lia shrugged. People publicly shied away from conversations about Helen's abilities, but they sure lined up whenever she offered free palm readings or gave away free dessert. Just one of the anomalies of Harvest. Palm reading and pie.

Lia flashed a wide grin before walking around the corner to her post office box, the heels of her boots clicking against the worn linoleum floor. She paused before opening the small door. Her breath hitched. She hoped just once she'd find a greeting card or postcard, something personal from someone who cared, even if that someone turned out to be her brother.

She turned the key in the lock. The small door opened. She bent to peer inside, only a flyer for pool products and a gun catalog. A quick stab of sadness shot to her chest. Happiness had taken a holiday and forgotten to write. If she wanted snail mail, she'd have to send it to herself. Gee, what fun that would be...and oh, so pathetic.

At the door, she waved good-bye to Zoë and hoped her smile appeared convincing.

Driving at the exact speed limit along tree-lined Main Street guaranteed a green light when she reached Fifth Avenue, the only intersection in town with a stoplight. The sheriff and his deputy staked it out on weekends, especially in the fall, to catch speeders or red-light runners—usually tourists headed for the only antique and what-not store for miles. They made exceptions for bus drivers delivering potential customers on their trips from Kansas City to Denver.

Lia rolled through a green light, passed the other streets, and turned left on Tenth.

"Townspeople have all day to shop," she muttered when cars filled all the parking spaces in front of the store. Today was the final day of the fall bulb sale. Garden club matrons wanted the best show of spring color around public spaces, which made the annual flower sale a big hit. Every year they planted existing gardens with more bulbs, replacing the ones squirrels and rabbits had munched on over the winter.

Lia raked her fingers through her shoulder length auburn hair, then fluffed her loose curls, the result of struggling with a curling iron. Steering the truck to the rear parking lot, she spied a too-familiar, battered blue pickup. Dread dropped free-fall into her stomach. She had no parachute to cushion the landing.

The last person she wanted to see was Lucas Dwyer.

****

Nothing but the arrival of his younger sister or madness would make Lucas brave Mr. Turner's farm store on Friday afternoon during the last day of the annual bulb sale.

"Excuse me, ma'am." Lucas bumped his way through the long line that began at the cash register and snaked around bins filled with toy tractors, rolled fleece blankets, and assorted tools. At six feet, he stood at least a head taller than the horde of women, mostly blue hairs, all chirping at once like parakeets in a cage. It reminded him of one of the few vacations his family took when he was a kid—he'd been lost at Bird World. He shuddered at the memory.

Near the back of the store, the manager worked at the key-making machine.

"Hey, Karl," Lucas shouted over the roar of the grinding wheel. "Did you have time to fill my order?"

Karl looked up and nodded before bending again to focus on the key.

Lucas checked his watch. He had time to kill before Craig arrived from St. Louis. Time to finish errands and grab a shower. Later, they'd visit Rockets, eat some barbecue, and hoist a few brews. But Craig would want a full report about Amelia. Lucas's gut tightened, twisting like someone wringing an old-fashioned mop. He'd never kept information from Craig before.

Glancing at the crowd, he spotted the corporate farm manager chatting up the very elderly Mrs. Watts. He wanted to hate the man for managing what should've been his farm, but in the end, the man had no fault. That man hadn't left his family and joined the Air Force after college. Guilt stabbed Lucas, a knife to his heart. He turned his attention to the array of plumbing supplies, but the pain of losing the farm rubbed like salt in a fresh wound. While he'd been away on active duty, his dad made some bad decisions, which over time cost them their farmstead. Their thousand acres, minus ten, now belonged to a corporation. At least they still held the title to their family home and the plot of land—free and clear. He had to remember that.

Karl shut off the grinder. "I've got that bag of stuff in the breakroom in the back." Karl grinned and looked him over, old black work boots, faded jeans, and chambray shirt torn at the elbow. "I never took you for that type of gardener, Combine."

Lucas rolled his eyes and followed Karl. Lucas didn't care for the nickname the guy had pinned on him. He'd started a combining company to harvest commercially when he left the Air Force, but there was more to him than farming. However, it seemed as though giving people silly nicknames was the only way Karl could remember who was who in Harvest. It wasn't that Karl wasn't a good guy. He just tried too hard to be country. After a month, he still oozed with city slickness. Plus, he mistakenly assumed all his neighbors were hicks—never been anywhere, never seen anything. Karl liked to jaw about his travels. Lucas had seen lots during college and nearly thirteen years of military service. He had nothing to prove. Karl seemed smart enough. He'd figure out who was who and what was what...or he'd leave, like Mr. Turner's other nephew who'd tried to run the farm store and failed to ever fit in.

In the back storeroom, away from the chaos of little old ladies and their chirping noises, Lucas paused as Karl plopped a big burlap bag onto an old wooden table and pointed.

"Crocuses and daffodils. I threw in some hostas, too. My thank-you to you for sort of teaching me the ropes about Harvest."

"They're for my sister," Lucas said, wondering where the urge to explain his purchase came from.

"Sister?"

He'd promised himself to maintain the homestead like his folks had before they moved to a retirement community in Arizona. He wanted his younger sister to have all the comforts of home when she visited from college, including flowerbeds filled with blooms in spring. To accomplish that required some replenishing each fall.

"Her name is Megan."

"Oh, sure," Karl replied. His smirk suggested he didn't believe a word of it. "I haven't seen her around."

"Well, you wouldn't. This isn't Manhattan, Kansas, or K-State. She's a student there. Only comes home once in a while." He wasn't about to explain the reason for her weekend homecoming—but come Sunday, the bulbs would work as a distraction. A time when they could plant side-by-side and talk about stuff. That worked best for them. They weren't ones to bare their souls to anyone, much less each other, but talking while working gave them a way to connect. And his way of keeping up with her without prying much.

Karl shifted his weight from one foot to the other. He looked down.

"What?" Lucas asked.

"Dude, is there more to do around here than Rockets on the weekend?"

"Sure, but most of it looks like farm work. Come to think of it, feels like farm work, too."

He hated being referred to as *Dude*. That offended him more than Combine.

"So what about..." Karl looked down again.

Lucas waited. If Karl had something more on his mind, he needed to spit it out. Guessing games were a waste of time, and he didn't have Helen Carter's mind-reading abilities.

Karl leaned in close. "What about the ladies?"

Lucas's brow wrinkled. "What about them?"

"Like, how do I get one? Seems there's all kinds of unwritten rules around here. Things you can say and do with one person that you can't say and do with another."

"Where'd you say you'd moved from?" Lucas asked.

"Chicago."

"Well, I don't know how things go in Chicago, but around here, you need to treat a female like a lady or you could have the whole town against you."

"But what about that Britton one? She's not really from around here, is she? Isn't she from Kansas City? Am I gonna step on anyone's toes if I ask her for a date?"

The punch to the gut surprised Lucas. His body stiffened. No one had ever referred to Amelia as *that Britton one* before. No, the man could not have a date with Amelia, but Karl wasn't exactly asking permission. Should he clue in the hardware store manager or let him discover the situation for himself? After all, Craig would arrive in a few hours. Amelia's brother would have plenty to say, in no uncertain terms, about why Karl, or any man from Harvest, shouldn't date his sister.

Before Lucas could answer, *click-clack* of boot heels against the tired linoleum echoed down the dimly lit hall.

"Karl?"

"Yah? In here."

Lucas groaned inwardly as Amelia stood framed in the doorway. He gritted his teeth but couldn't stop from staring. She'd lost her farm-work clothes—baggy overalls and grungy t-shirt—replaced them with a curve-hugging denim skirt, a sexy top, and she glowed like her face was lit by a spotlight. Her hair hung in loose waves around her face. She had haunted his dreams, and now she haunted his personal space.

"Speak of the devil," Karl murmured and bumped his elbow against Lucas's side. Lucas grunted.

"Hey! How are you? What can I help you with?" Karl

asked taking a step forward.

Lucas caught Amelia's frown, which she quickly lifted into a wide smile, aiming it at Karl. "I can come back another time. I didn't know you were busy. Mr. Turner said I would find you back here, but again, I didn't know you were with a customer."

"Amelia." Lucas nodded to her. He wouldn't allow her to ignore him, and if he hadn't been watching for it, her return nod could've been missed.

"Amelia? I thought your name was Lia Britton." Karl's expression turned puzzled as he looked at Lucas, then to Lia, and back to Lucas again.

She smiled sweetly. "My given name is Amelia, but no one calls me that anymore."

"Only family," Lucas bit out more harshly than intended.

"Huh?" Karl asked. "You two related?"

"No!" Lia snapped as if poked with a cattle prod. Her brown eyes glowered as though she wanted to stab him with one.

"Craig will be here by dinner." Lucas kept his voice low and even.

"Your boyfriend?" Karl asked, looking worried.

"Brother," Lucas said at the same time as Lia.

"Oh." Karl relaxed, flexing his shoulders. "In that case, I was wondering if you'd like to go out tomorrow night."

"No," Lucas said.

"I wasn't asking *you*," Karl snapped.

"Doesn't matter. She's got plans tomorrow."

Lia scowled so hard that if she'd had special, super-hero powers Lucas was certain his eyebrows and lashes would be singed, probably burned off his face.

"Karl, I'm sorry, but I do have a longstanding engagement for tomorrow. However," she brightened, "I came to ask *you* if you would like to go out next Saturday night? There's a bistro on the river in Atchison. I thought we might go there."

"Yeah. I'd like that." Karl perked up like a strutting rooster in a yard full of hens. "What time shall I pick you up?"

Lucas frowned. "Amelia, Craig's not going to like this."

The end of Chapter 1

If you've enjoyed meeting Lia and Lucas in **Her Heart's Desire**, please consider picking up the book at your favorite online retail outlet.

Christmas Bells

Dear Reader,

I hope you will fall in love with Chalise and Chaz in *Behind the Mask*. There are other folks in the cast you might enjoy, too, like Billy, Win, Doucetta, and Gator. The setting is a fictional Mississippi River town in Louisiana, specifically in Ascension Parish. However, there is no town named Ascension. It exists only in my imagination.

Tennessee Williams wrote in *A Streetcar Named Desire*, "Oh, you can't describe someone you're in love with!" However, I hope I've done an adequate job of describing Ascension, along with its culture and customs. You see, I love Louisiana. My roots run deep there. After all, it's where my people are buried.

In hopes of making your reading experience more enjoyable, I'm adding a list of terms to make the vernacular of everyday-speak in Louisiana a bit easier. These explanations are short and sweet, but like Louisiana, there is more to know if you wish to dig deeper.

Carnival: A season of revelry beginning on January 6, or **Twelfth Night**, and ending on Fat Tuesday or Mardi Gras. There are weekly parties and parades. How long it lasts is determined by a bit of complicated computations. See Mardi Gras.

Flambeaux Carrier: People who carry gas torches or "Flambeaux" to light the streets for parading krewes. A tradition that began during Carnival in the late 1830s in New Orleans.

Krewe: A krewe is an organization formed to host a

110

Mardi Gras ball and produce a Mardi Gras parade complete with floats. Members often participate in social events held throughout the year. For example, there are about sixty different krewes in New Orleans, and each one hosts a parade. They "roll" or parade on a certain date or dates during Carnival Season. Not every krewe rolls on Fat Tuesday.

Laissez les bons temps rouler: Let the good times roll!

Makin' groceries: It means you are going to go buy groceries.

Mardi Gras: Fat Tuesday. Tuesday before Ash Wednesday, the day marking the beginning of the Lenten season. How is all that calculated? Easter falls on the first Sunday **after** the first full moon of the vernal equinox, or after March 21. Mardi Gras is usually set about 47 days before Easter. This means that the actual date of Mardi Gras changes from year to year.

Second Line: A Second Line is a parade led by a brass band—the main line. The folks who follow behind are the second line, but they're not marching with any precision. Instead, revelers wave handkerchiefs and twirl parasols. Dancers are buck-jumping. (It's a dance. If you check the blog on my website, I have video of this. A picture is worth a thousand words. I can't explain the steps, though if you saw the PBS special of Harry Connick, Jr. preforming at the Lincoln Center a few years ago, he demonstrated it.) A Second Line can be part of a main parade at a big festival celebration, or it can be as simple as a neighborhood band gathering to parade and locals joining in or standing on their porches cheering the parade on. Its historical roots are connected to funerals.

Throws: Beads, balls, and other sorts of doodads are thrown by krewe members from floats. Some krewes specialize in their throws, such as the Krewe of Zulu always has coconuts. In 1870 is the first known record of Mardi Gras "throws."

Twelfth Night: January 6th. The twelfth night after Christmas. This is a constant date. It doesn't change like the date of Mardi Gras. It is the start of the **Carnival Season**.

There are many other words, phrases, and traditions connected with Mardi Gras. Check my blog on my website www.linda-joyce.com for more Louisiana and Mardi Gras traditions.

Happy Reading!
Linda Joyce

Behind The Mask

By

Linda Joyce

Chapter One

Chalise gazed into a full-length cheval mirror in her
bedroom. She tried not to fuss anymore with her outfit. Biting
her lower lip, she banked on no one recognizing her in the belly
dancing costume after more than ten years away from home.
Purple, green, and gold beads draped from a sequined top and
covered her torso. Gossamer gold silk harem pants hid her legs.
She selected purple leather ballet slippers rather than heels to
minimize her height. All to distract. All to create an illusion.

Adjusting a purple mask studded with shiny rhinestones,
she smiled at the end result. It hid the upper half of her face
while a gauzy veil concealed the bottom half. She chose this
mask, this costume, and planned a late arrival to Ascension's
Twelfth Night celebration taking place at the Civic Center.
Sneaking into town was necessary to her plan for reentry into
local society, but it still required every last grain of her
courage. Nervousness again skittered through her veins.

Soon news of her return would spread through town the
same way fireworks light up a night sky. A few days to settle in
would steel her backbone against the barrage of questions sure
to come her way. After all, other than her father's funeral, she
hadn't returned to Ascension in over ten years.

Sucking in a breath, she blew it out. The veil ruffled with
the exhale. Regardless of what happened in the next few weeks,

she'd hold her chin high. Moving back didn't mean she'd tucked her pride like a tail between her legs. Modeling had run its course. The constant dieting and need to look perfect for a camera—it loved heroin chic—no longer held any appeal. No one had asked her, but in her opinion, she looked better with the ten pounds she'd gained. If her father was alive, he'd agree.

As long as she smiled and exuded confidence, people would believe anything about why she left New York. In truth, she had a good run, waved her own checkered flag, then left for a variety of reasons. But in the near future, a press release would announce the tranquil and rejuvenating qualities of her new salon and spa, Sanctuary, which is what Ascension was to her. Hopefully, only a few people would seek to scratch away the veneer she'd polished and presented to the world, and she counted on her upstanding reputation to pull her through pointed questions.

Peeking through the window, she noticed the headlights of a hired car, the chariot to take her to the party. She had arranged for the ride to pick her up behind the house as the front entrance was mainly used by guests. Out of necessity, her mother had converted their mansion into Boudreau Bed and Breakfast. It still bugged Chalise to find strangers in residence in the family bedrooms.

"You want to go to the Civic Center, right?" the driver asked. "The party has already started."

Not daring to speak, lest the man recognize her, she handed him written confirmation of her destination. Jimmy Folse had shared the same microscope with her during ninth-grade biology. He'd be on the radio to dispatch bragging to everyone about driving her around.

"If you want a ride back to the B&B, give me a call, and

I'll pick you up," he told her when she paid the tab in cash. She nodded, but had already arranged a ride home with her mother's fiancé.

Once inside the cavernous arena, music pulsed, and lights flashed. The DJ spun his magic. Chalise moved to the music as she slipped through the crowd gathered around the perimeter of the dance floor ever vigilant that someone might recognize her. Scoping out the scene, she safely took in every detail of each person from behind the safe anonymity of her mask, and her wariness diminished. She recognized so many friends from high school. Memories, mostly good ones, flooded through her. They didn't know she'd kept tabs on them through weekly phone calls home. Homesickness never entirely left her when she lived in New York. Over the years since high school, Momma had provided the lowdown about the matching up between her friends and classmates.

When a waiter passed with a tray loaded with flutes of champagne, Chalise snagged one to moisten her parched throat. She sipped slowly. It gave her an excuse to put off several men and a woman who asked her to dance. With each invitation, she shook her head. In a few weeks, when she met them at a Chamber of Commerce meeting or at the grocery store, would they laugh if they discovered it was she they'd hit on?

"Happy Twelfth Night, y'all," the DJ shouted an hour after her arrival. "This is the last dance." The lights dimmed. The mirrored balls throughout the arena spun. Following tradition, a classic song began to play. Donna Summer singing *McArthur Park*.

"Last dance." Voices blended and grew louder.

A hand grabbed hers and lifted the champagne glass away. A pirate pulled her to the dance floor. She started to protest, but nearby Doucetta, Mary, Pratt, and Gaurou, all old schoolmates, tapped their feet to the music and looked on, grins spread across their faces. If she spoke in protest, they would recognize her voice, so she allowed her captor the last dance. After all, who said no to a rakish pirate? Black knee-high boots, dark gray breeches, and a white shirt with billowing sleeves. An ostrich feather in his black hat waved as he moved. An eye patch hid one eye. In the dimness and the flashes of mirrored light, she couldn't quite decide if they'd met before.

She draped her arms around his neck. As she reached her fingers to run through his thick hair, her captor twirled her way, and then pulled her close. The attention from the mystery man wasn't without allure. He moved well. Oozed charm. Tingling sensations left her breathless.

Her hand was warmed by his. Each time her gaze lingered on his face, he twirled her away. It was as though he somehow sensed her intention to determine his identity.

Halfway through the song, he danced with her cheek to cheek. Broad shoulders. Well-developed muscled arms. Narrow waist. Strong thighs. They swayed together. All thoughts took flight as she found comfort in his arms. When the song neared its end, the pirate's hand slipped from the small of her back to her butt. He gave a light squeeze. She sucked in a breath and stopped.

"How dare you," she hissed.

The pirate's hands moved up to her neck. He cupped her jaw, and then he brought his lips to hers. Though a thin veil separated skin-on-skin contact, the heat of his lips seared. The electric zip dazed her.

"I've waited years to do this, Princess," the pirate

whispered.

Her hands flew to her cheeks, and she touched her lips with her fingers. Fear struck. Would he reveal her identity? How did he know?

The pirate removed his feathered hat. He bowed deeply, and taking one of her hands, he kissed it. A second later, he turned and melted into the crowd as the last note of the song rang out through the Civic Center.

"Chaz Riboucheaux," she squeaked. The last man she wanted to see tonight. She wouldn't put herself in the position of being made a fool a second time. The first time, more than ten years ago, was quite enough. No matter how much her mother sang his praises now.

* * *

"Dammit, Billy!" Chaz shouted. "You can't charge a thousand dollars for champagne to the company." He smacked the invoice lying on his desk, then snatched it up. Stalking down the hall of the single-wide trailer that served as the temporary office of Action Enterprises, he passed Lisa, their shared secretary, in the receiving room. Without knocking, he strode into the office of William Rutherford Salanger IV at the opposite end.

Before he had a chance to utter a word, Billy raised a finger gesturing for silence as he finished his phone call. Chaz paused his rant.

"Yes, Councilman, Mr. W. R. Salanger the third *is* my father. No, my company isn't affiliated with any of his holdings." Billy laughed. "I don't ride my family's coattails. That's not how Salangers do things. This is my company"—

Chaz narrowed his eyes and glared at Billy as he continued his conversation— "mine *and* my business partner's."

Chaz locked his jaw at Billy's placating smile.

"Our company has a lot to offer the city of Ascension. We want to see it grow and be a part of helping it prosper." Billy straightened the knot of his tie, a move Chaz had seen a million times before his friend went in for the kill. "We're not a hit-and-run operation. I assure you, we will be an exceptional corporate citizen for years to come."

Billy nodded at something the Councilman said. Then he responded, "The offer for a round of golf at River Bend with you and two of your staff is still open. We're quite proud of the improvements to the course…Friday at 9:00 a.m. it is."

Billy hung up the phone and leaned back in his chair, moving his hands behind his neck and lifting his Gucci loafer-clad feet to the top of his desk. "Who says deals aren't still made on the golf course?"

"Fine," Chaz muttered, then moved papers from the corner of Billy's desk, and parked there. "But why buy the most expensive champagne for our party last week? We got a few lookers, but no solid investors in the condo project for the golf course."

"Priming the pump, bro. You know how I operate. We're putting this town at a bend in the Mississippi River on the map."

"You sound like an infomercial."

"And speaking of operating"—Billy pointed a finger at him—"those were some smooth moves at that Twelfth Night gig. You said she was pretty. A tad understated, don't you think? Tall. Thin. Moves gracefully. Gorgeous."

Chaz forced a laugh. "She's business. Priming the pump

119

as you call it."

"I did a little background check on the lovely *Miss* Chalise Boudreau."

"Stay out of my business."

"Not so fast." Billy's feet moved to the floor, and he leaned over his desk. "What involves you, involves me. Moving here to start a company with you, I knew what I was getting. But *she* brings a new slant to things you never mentioned."

"None of your business. And this is *my* business. I own fifty-five percent."

"What if I want to prime her pump?"

"No," Chaz snapped, resisting the urge to wipe the sly grin off Billy's face. The last thing Billy needed to know was his history with Chalise. "We agreed not to mix business with pleasure. I set you up as the front man for my company to accomplish something here. In case you've forgotten, your monthly trust fund stipend requires you to be gainfully employed. I allowed you to invest. Our benefactor might be your grandmother, but I'm the one giving you the opportunity of a lifetime when no one else will have you. Mess with Chalise, and our deal is dead. Null. Void. She's a means to an end. That's all."

"Hey now, I'm making progress on some of these deals— inroads with your townsfolk. I get to have a little fun now and then. You knew going in my…desire for southern hospitality."

"Yeah, I admit, your name and your charm have opened some doors, but after nearly nine months of work, the mayor still refuses to meet with me," Chaz pointed out. "We want him and the entire council to see things our way with the *Magnolia May*. We need that lease. End of story."

120

"So, we'll invite the mayor to be the guest of honor at the ribbon cutting ceremony for the ship. Back to the woman. The New York model."

"I told you."

"She made plenty of money at one time. Why is she here?" Billy asked. "No offense, but Ascension has two classes of people—the wealthy and the help. Then, there are the transient tourists. I know she doesn't fit into one of those pockets."

"You're a snob."

Billy shrugged. "You've always known that about me."

"Chalise has history here. Her family was once the richest in town. Her father built the mansion that's now Boudreau B&B. But while Mrs. Boudreau has never said, I'm guessing he left a river of debt, which is why she went from socialite to businesswoman. Her mother has developed a soft spot for me, wanting to right an old wrong, she says. No idea what she means, but I'm going with it. We're making headway with local society through Mrs. Boudreau's connections as the Chamber President. And, as I said before, Chalise Boudreau is my ticket to respectability. Remember, I come from a family who wasn't good enough to clean the shoes of those you label 'the help.' And you're wrong about Ascension. There is a thriving middle class, and they're our target market. They're the heartbeat of this place. Not the society rich."

"So what's your plan, man? She's refused to take your calls. You sent a bouquet of flowers. She sent them back. How do you plan to get beyond the moat surrounding her? What the hell did you do to her in the past?"

Chaz rose. "Nothing." He raised a warning eyebrow. "You work your plan. I'll work mine. But just so we're clear, she's off limits to you."

He turned and strode out of Billy's office with the ring of his business partner's laughter following him down the hall. "I'll get to the bottom of this thing between the two of you," he shouted. "I'm good at solving puzzles."

Chaz was done playing nice with Chalise. His once bad-boy reputation had attracted her, drew her to him like a fish to bait when she was still in high school. The aloofness she showed to the world was a façade. Behind it beat the heart of a do-gooder, raising money for a variety of charities and even volunteering at the animal shelter. She'd let down her royal guard for the tough guy who skirted the law and thumbed his nose at rules. On to plan B. He could revive a bit of his bad-boy ways, throw in a bit of finesse—whatever it took to get Chalise's undivided attention. Ten years ago, she'd taken his heart, cut him out of her life, and yet, it still only beat for her.

"Princess," he said, reaching his office chair and settling into it. "I've got a deal for you. One you won't be able to refuse."

End of Chapter 1

If you've enjoyed the story so far, please consider picking up the book at one of the online retail outlets.

For news on upcoming books, events, and giveaways, please sign up for Linda's newsletter, **LETTERS from Linda**. http://eepurl.com/4y5Yj

Connect with Linda on Social Media
Website: http://www.linda-joyce.com
Facebook: https://www.facebook.com/LindaJoyceAuthor
Twitter: @LJWriter
Goodreads:
http://www.goodreads.com/author/show/6950241.Linda_Joyce
Pinterest: Linda Joyce Worlds.

YouTube: https://www.youtube.com/channel/UCrjZh-TMFbeN1k7BlWAAxeA

Amazon Author Page
http://www.amazon.com/Linda-Joyce/e/B00BODDROS/

Amazon UK author page:
https://www.amazon.co.uk/Linda-Joyce/e/B00BODDROS/ref=sr_ntt_srch_lnk_5?qid=1477665604&sr=8-5

About Linda

Linda Joyce is an Amazon Best Selling author and 4-time RONE Award Finalist with a smattering of other awards who writes about assertive females and the men who can't resist them. She has penned the Fleur de Lis series, Fleur de Lis Brides series, and the Sunflower series. Her other books include Behind the Mask and Christmas Bells.

A big fan of jazz and blues, Linda attributes her love of those musical genres to her southern roots, which run deep in Louisiana. If you walk through several New Orleans cemeteries you'll find many of her people buried there. She's lived coast to coast curtesy of her father's Air Force career. She wrote her first manuscript when she was twelve while living in Japan, the country where her mother was born and raised. In addition to being a book addict, Linda's a foodie, an RVer, loves to kayak, and binge watch movies. Now she lives in Atlanta, Georgia with her husband and General Beauregard, their four-legged boy.

www.ingramcontent.com/pod-product-compliance
Lightning Source LLC
Chambersburg PA
CBHW060623130626
46555CB00002B/639